BOTS
DEGREES OF FREEDOM

Nicole M. Taylor

EPIC
Press

Degrees of Freedom
Bots: Book #4

Written by Nicole M. Taylor

Copyright © 2016 by Abdo Consulting Group, Inc.

Published by EPIC Press™
PO Box 398166
Minneapolis, MN 55439

Cover design by Dorothy Toth
Images for cover art obtained from iStockPhoto.com
Edited by Jennifer Skogen

Library of Congress Cataloging-in-Publication Data

Taylor, Nicole M.
Degrees of freedom / Nicole M. Taylor.
p. cm. — (Bots ; #4)
Summary: When Shannon Liao sees an internet video of a man doing what seems
to be impossible, she finds a rabbit-hole of human-Bot interaction, extreme body
modification and, possibly, the solution to all her problems.
ISBN 978-1-68076-004-0 (hardcover)
1. Robots—Fiction. 2. Robotics—Fiction. 3. Young adult fiction. I. Title.
[Fic]—dc23
2015932714

EPICPRESS.COM

"Degrees of Freedom": *Def. The specific modes in which a mechanical object may move. The more dimensions a robot occupies, the more degrees of freedom exist.*

ONE

THE MAN IN THE VIDEO

And once again, Shannon Liao had found herself in the unenviable position of being (mostly) sober while everyone around her tripped extravagantly.

She told Felix that it wouldn't work. She had been taking anti-anxiety medication since she was eleven years old. Almost every year, she'd had to up her dosage as her tolerance increased. Now, at nearly twenty-two, she was practically un-fuck-up-able. She rarely got drunk, she'd never been high, and though Felix had assured her that mushrooms were the thing ("All natural!"), her failure to feel anything now hardly surprised her.

"They look like dehydrated dog turds," she pointed out. Felix, lying next to her on the soft grass, just chuckled absently to himself. His girlfriend, a chubby, petite sociology major, rested her head on his stomach, occasionally reaching up to poke him delicately. He didn't seem to notice.

"Just relax," Felix said. That's what he always said. If Shannon could relax at will, she wouldn't have this problem in the first place. "Don't eat any more of them." Shannon hadn't planned on it. She'd already made that mistake at her first big college party freshman year, pounding sticky, sickly jager bombs in a futile bid to give herself a buzz. Instead, she spent the night in the communal shower trying to aim her stream of vomit directly into the drain.

On her other side, the goggle-eyed young man whom she knew vaguely from an anthropology seminar last semester sat cross-legged, staring down at his own intertwined fingers. Shannon didn't know where Felix found these people, or how he knew for sure that they were trustworthy. If Felix could hear what was going on inside her head, he would tell her that she was being ridiculous—no one cared about a few 'shrooms.

Shannon slumped back on the cold grass and focused on controlling her breathing. It was a strategy her therapist had given her. She was to breathe carefully in through her nose and then exhale through her mouth with a mindful "ahhhh" sound. Shannon counted her breaths, focused on the feeling of her lungs expanding, and looked up at the sky through a lacy filigree of tree branches.

The park wasn't technically on campus—it belonged to the city, not the school. But it was so close that almost anywhere Shannon looked, she saw students, throwing chip remnants to the ducks, jogging around the edge of the lake, sunning themselves with textbooks opened uselessly beside them.

Finals week had brought out all the chattering young people, burdens easing off their shoulders as the year came to a close. Shannon herself had completed all of her finals. She didn't even have any real exams this year, just a series of projects. She was confident she had done well; she generally did. It all came so easy to her, languages were intuitive, like a muscle-memory.

Before, Shannon had always been at peace with the end of the school year. It meant a lull time, either heading back home or, more likely, to some internship or to her part-time waitressing gig, if nothing else. This was the first year that finals week had triggered that familiar sick-and-fluttery feeling deep in her guts because, for the first time, there was nothing after finals week.

Well, there were actually several things afterwards. Her lease was up in September. Grad school applications were due in December. Her student access to the language labs and the campus library was deactivated in January. It was a staggered series of endings and it suddenly seemed to Shannon that they were all coming too fast.

She poked her elbow out, nudged Felix in the

shoulder. "Are you gonna leave the apartment after commencement?"

Felix had been Shannon's suite-mate freshman year. At first, they had approached one another with a reserved wariness, like two dogs passing in the street. Over time, though, they had developed a kind of rapport. Felix was the one who had nursed Shannon through that jager-bomb incident, in fact. He was easygoing where she was high-strung, shy where she was enthusiastic, thoughtful where she was impulsive. They evened one another out. They worked so well together, in fact, that they had lived together in one situation or another for all of undergrad. When September came the lease would be up and she had to decide whether to renew with a new roommate or move somewhere else. Either way, it would be the first time in her adult life that Shannon lived somewhere without Felix.

"I'm not going to commencement," Felix said, his voice dreamy and vague. "Mom wants me to visit relatives in Chennai, then I'm going right from there up to Washington." A graphic designer, Felix already had a position with an indie firm up in Seattle. His life was on track and he would proceed in an orderly fashion from academia to the working world, as they were all supposed to be doing.

It seemed it was just Shannon who was flailing.

"Shit," Shannon said."You got it all figured out, huh?"

Felix just shrugged. His girlfriend struggled to sit up. She smacked her lips as though they were dry, and grimaced slightly. "Is anyone else having . . . weird colors?" she asked.

Shannon pointed at her head as if to say: *My crazy brain, am I right?*

"Aw," Felix's girlfriend said, reaching out a hand to touch Shannon's cheek. Shannon quirked an eyebrow at her and the girl looked at her own hand, as if wondering how it had found itself in such a strange position. "I have no idea why I did that," she began to giggle. Shannon couldn't help but laugh along with her.

Shannon tried to remember what Felix's girl-friend did for a living—she wasn't a student. The girlfriend was new, as evidenced by the fact that she still registered in Shannon's head as "Felix's girlfriend" rather than . . . Julie? June? J-something.

The good thing about stoned people, though, was that they were generally quite forgiving of social faux-pas, so Shannon felt quite comfortable asking: "Hey, what is your name?"

"Ha!" the girl said. "Elia."

Elia. So much for "J" then.

"Elia, what are you going to do now that Felix is going to Seattle?" Elia was doing something with the long grass, plaiting into a green braid.

"I dunno," she said. "Maybe I'll go with him. I don't mind the rain."

Shannon nodded sagely. It would be nice to have someone to move for. Someone to take direction from.

"I'm going to Northwestern," said the guy from

the anthropology seminar. Shannon had forgotten he was still with them. "Going for my masters."

He had his shit together then. He wasn't even giving himself the customary few months of rootlessness before frantically filling out grad school applications in a blind panic. Grad school. That was what Shannon's father wanted her to do and he was hardly subtle about it. She hadn't called him in six weeks because she was tired of all his little "reminders" about deadlines and references and writing samples. For some reason, he was in love with the idea of his daughter as a distinguished academic.

Elia had started twining the grass-braid into her own hair. It stuck out at odd angles.

"You should backpack through . . . somewhere," Elia advised. Shannon laughed. Her father would only tolerate a certain level of dithering. He definitely would not be cool with Shannon putting her "career" on hold to . . . whatever around in Olde Europe or something.

"Nah, Dad would kill me." Shannon stretched her arms out on either side of her body. Grass-angels. "What I need is a fucking J-O-B."

Elia patted her shoulder. "You'll find something."

Elia was awfully confident for someone who knew nothing about Shannon. Probably *because* she knew nothing about Shannon. Linguistics was the deadest of ends. It was like majoring in Dodo bird grooming or auto parts manufacturing. And it had happened so quickly, too. From her freshman year to her senior year, Bot technology had exploded, filling in the gaps in human linguistic ability like spackle. Human interpreters and translators were nearly obsolete. Even the military, which had always been hungry for multi-lingual people, no longer prioritized language skills above any other aptitude.

Not that Shannon necessarily wanted to join the Army or anything. But it had always been there in the back of her head, a cushion of nepotism and familiarity. Now even that was gone.

"I should have majored in building fucking Bots," Shannon mused. "That's what everyone wants."

Felix straightened his arm, pointing it at the clouds above them. "Damn straight!" he said, so loud that some of the ducks gliding along on the lake swiveled to look accusatorially at them.

"I think I know a Bot," Elia said, so quietly that, at first, Shannon thought she might have hallucinated it—her first instance of any effect from the mushrooms.

"Like a TA?" Shannon asked. Legally, students were not permitted to be alone with the SennTech TAs at any time and they had very rigid programming when it came to classroom instruction. Most people thought of them as something like a projector or a supersized flex-tablet—another piece of equipment. No one really "knew" a Bot.

Elia shook her head, lips tucked in tight in a worried little kiss gesture.

"No, I don't think he's . . . " She waved her

hand in front of her face. "Never mind. I'm high as shit."

The anthropology guy had bent over until his face skimmed the grass. He moved his nose gently amongst the green blades. Felix's eyes were closed. Maybe he was sleeping. Shannon leaned toward the other girl and smiled. "We're all alone," she said, "you can tell me."

Elia's eyes were big and credulous, wheedling her felt a little bit like manipulating a child. As the involuntarily designated Sober Person at every party, Shannon had encountered this feeling before every time she tricked someone out of their keys or replaced someone's glass with one full of water.

"I don't think I'm supposed to know," Elia said. At some point, she had started rocking back and forth very slightly, just inches in either direction. She didn't seem to be aware of her movements.

Shannon drew her pinched fingers along the seam of her lips. At the corner of her mouth, she pretended to turn an invisible key. "I'm trustworthy," Shannon said. "Ask anyone. Ask Felix."

Elia nodded deeply at this, mollified. "Felix says you're good people."

During her forward arc, she leaned further and further, until her forehead was resting against Shannon's cheekbone. For a second, Shannon wasn't sure if this was a deliberate movement or simply a controlled fall. And then she began to hiss into her ear.

"At the pizza place where I work, there's this guy. I think he's one of . . . them. You know, the other ones. Not a SennTech."

Shannon pulled back slightly, confused. Elia clung to her shoulder as though it were the only thing keeping her off the ground. "SennTech is the only company—"

Elia chuckled so low in her throat that she didn't even open her mouth. "Nah. There's other ones. Better ones. They keep 'em a secret because they're so good . . . They're so good, they're gonna replace us. The government is testing it out," Elia leaned back up and whispered in the general direction of Shannon, "covertly."

Shannon laughed and set Elia upright. After the scare a couple of years ago about the so-called Hart Series Bots that the Army was working on, every loony with a blog was railing about how super-robots were infiltrating society. "That's a little 'tinfoil hat,' don't you think?" she said. Shannon's father rarely talked about his work, but he had grown so much more resigned and tense since the big Bot scandal with that dude—Edward something?—that Shannon assumed, like everyone else, that the Army's robotics program was being phased out. They certainly weren't posting Bots in college-town pizza places.

"Look it up!" Elia's voice was suddenly far too loud. Felix's eyes fluttered open. The anthropology guy just pushed his face deeper into the grass. Shannon thought he must have been touching dirt at that point.

"Okay," Shannon said, "I will."

———o———

She didn't. At least, not right away. There was too much to do in the days approaching commencement. After Felix left, Shannon had no one to talk to and about three months of rent to cover. She put the apartment up on all sorts of rental websites and spent most of her free time fielding offers. Well, that and avoiding calls from her father.

He probably just wanted to finalize travel details for commencement but Shannon had developed what she thought of as a "nerve bundle" around communications with him. When her cell phone rang she felt a cold seizing of panic in her stomach. When an e-mail popped up, her breaths grew shallow and erratic. She spent long hours doing nothing in particular—playing time-waster games, reading stupid articles, taking quizzes to determine which large breed of dog she was—to avoid actually meeting those unanswered missives head-on.

One night, at the end of a long avoidance jag,

she found herself clicking through an endless succession of videos. She'd started with a video of a kitten getting lost in a ski boot and, somehow, had wound up watching one about reptoid aliens (LOCAL POLITICIAN HAS DOUBLE EYELID! THEY CANNOT HIDE). In the "recommended videos" in the sidebar, there was one simply called BOT MALFUNCTION. It was dated more than a year and a half ago. Despite that, it only had about seven hundred views.

Shannon hadn't thought much about what Elia had told her. It didn't surprise her that there would be all sorts of conspiracy theories about robots. No one knew how to deal with them. The SennTech Bots were all over the news and it seemed like people were constantly writing think-pieces about what Bots meant for the human condition or whatever. The Army had screwed the pooch, trying to launch their own line of uber-realistic Bots before discovering that they were wildly defective and not nearly as human as they were supposed to be. That had made a lot of hay for late-night comedians. People always seemed ready to believe any level of intelligent malfeasance even when common-as-dirt incompetence was staring them right in the face.

She clicked on the video. It was amateur footage from someone's flex tablet, the person kept zooming in way too far and blurring the image. It looked like some sort of restaurant or coffee shop or something and she could hear people speaking in the background. The voices were muffled, but she could make out enough to guess that they were speaking French.

For the first forty-eight seconds, the cameraperson skulked around the edges of a knot of people who had collected in the back of the room. There were shouting and loud clattering sounds coming from somewhere in front of the gathering of people, and the cameraperson was clearly trying to get a good angle. Eventually, the person behind the camera just muscled aside a girl who looked to be about eleven or twelve.

"Nice," Shannon chuckled to herself.

Inside the circle, a young man was sitting placidly with his feet flat on the floor and a small white plate in his hands. "It's a defect," he said conversationally to no one in particular. He spoke English with a generic newscaster accent. "My fear response is triggered by normal stimuli. That's an error, right? That's faulty wiring."

He smiled cheerfully, still not looking at anyone in particular. "But that can be fixed. That is our only birthright: we can be fixed. We can fix ourselves, even."

It was hard to hear the last part because, as he spoke, he slapped the plate against the floor, breaking it into a number of fat shards. He held one, triangular and relatively sharp, against his own skull, right above his left eyebrow.

An uneasy murmur moved through the little crowd and whoever was holding the flex-tablet trembled slightly. Then, before anyone could react, the man took the plate shard and dug it deep into his skin. Deeper, it seemed, than anyone could tolerate without crying out.

The shard wasn't sharp enough to cut cleanly so he had to drag it through his flesh, tearing rather than slicing. Blood streamed out of the wound and puddled on the gathered cloth of his shirt.

Someone screamed.

The man reached up and grabbed the hanging edge of his torn skin. He took it firmly in his fist and gave an almighty pull.

"*Putain,*" someone called out and then the picture went completely to shit. It looked like the cameraperson as well as a few other people leapt forward to restrain the man. Everything became a tangle of shade and light. And then black.

As soon as the video was over, Shannon clicked on the uploader's name. There was nothing in their "About Me" section, and no description of the video. It was the only video they had uploaded. The comments did not offer any more enlightenment:

how did i get here? i was watching makeup vids and then . . .

hahahahahha . . . so metal

definitely faked. Blood doesn't look like that. OP is full of shit.

humans cant do that

Shannon felt . . . something, a little lingering . . . something. Like the mental equivalent of a popcorn-kernel stuck in one of her teeth. That last comment . . .

She knew, of course, that humans were capable of all manner of horrible depredations perpetrated on both themselves and others, given the right circumstances. That guy was probably just some poor mentally ill person who wandered into this café and cried for help in a particularly spectacular way.

That was probably the right answer. But it wasn't satisfying her completely. So Shannon did a little basic Googling. She felt pretty confident that the café was in Europe, at least based on the type of crockery in the video. The audio quality hadn't been great, but she hadn't been able to recognize any particularly intrusive regional accents, so that probably meant a larger city in France. Or Francophone Belgium.

She tried searching for a few keywords in French and English ("tore skin," "mentally ill," "coffee-shop," "American") and came up with nothing at all. It was, Shannon admitted, a quixotic quest. She didn't have any names or even a place for sure. This could have happened in some tiny town somewhere and the local newspaper just wasn't digitized. That was probably it.

But the popcorn kernel of the mind remained.

When Shannon finally exhausted herself use-lessly flittering around the Internet, she slept hard and dreamt in disconnected scraps. She thought she might have dreamed about the man in the café, but it was hard to remember. Everything blurred together and people were not who they were, or they were more than one person at once. She forgot a lot. The one thing she remembered, upon waking, was his voice when he had said: "We can be fixed. We can fix ourselves."

TWO

A PLACE TO LAND

FORT COWIN, CA. FEBRUARY, 2047

There was one fatal flaw in his plan: no one picked up hitchhikers anymore. Especially not lone young men, though Edmond hardly thought of himself as a threatening presence. He'd gotten his most recent ride from a woman in her twenties. The right side of her head was cleanly shaved, the left side was a long slim braid. She looked at him as though almost daring him to come over the armrest at her. She agreed to drop him on the other side of the California border if he'd cover the gas. She wasn't, thank God, a talker and it had been a very pleasant one hundred thirty miles, listening to her playlist labeled "Get the FUCK outta Dodge."

"Hey," she said, when she left him at a large truck stop complete with restaurant and pay-for-use showers, "you should get off the road. You're gonna get hurt out here, okay?"

Bemused, Edmond thanked her and handed over the last portion of gas money he'd promised her. Before she left, she winked at him.

She was probably the nicest driver he'd encountered. One person threw a crumpled styrofoam food container at him. Or possibly they were just throwing out the container and Edmond happened to be standing in its path. Most of the cars weren't driven by humans at all; he saw an enormous number of driverless cars, their occupants dozing like children in the backseat or working busily on flex-tablets. Those cars, he assumed, were not programmed to stop outside of their predetermined destinations.

After giving the braid girl gas money, Edmond had six—no—seven dollars left on him. Enough for a sandwich, maybe. The restaurant portion of the truck stop emanated a wan yellow glow, the huge glass front revealing a stunning dearth of customers. When he went inside, he didn't even see so much as a waitress.

The only other human being in the place was a slumped figure leaning into the corner of a green faux-leather booth. The person's arms and hands were tucked inside their big down jacket, and the hood was pulled low over their face. Edmond sat down at the table across from the person and regarded the half-empty bottle of ketchup and the color-coded packets of sugar and sugar-substitutes.

The slumped person had a set of silverware in front of them but no plate or glass. Still no waitress in sight.

"Is this place . . . open?" Edmond asked the figure, who may have, he realized, actually been asleep. Or dead.

But she wasn't. He could see now that the figure was a woman because she moved slightly and made her reflection visible in the glass next to her face. She looked as though she were about his age or a little older, but that it had been a rough road getting there.

"Yeah," she said, her voice hoarse from disuse, "they just slow."

She adjusted the hood of her jacket into a make-shift pillow and leaned against the windowpane. For a moment, there was silence. Edmond did not find it uncomfortable, but apparently the woman did, because she added, "I think it's her break."

"Oh," Edmond said, not having any other comment. "I'll . . . wait, then."

The woman sighed and sat up straighter. She pushed back her hood and looked at Edmond sourly, as though he had forced her into an exchange of small talk. "I saw you come in with that Prius," she said. "You hitch-hiking?"

With her hood folded down, he could see that she had a thin yet improbably jowly face with dark brown hair in a low ponytail. A swirling dot of gray on the top of her head revealed her dye job. Her face was spotted with large freckles and she wore no makeup, except for a shockingly pink smear of lipstick on her mouth. She had rings on all of her fingers, most of them looked like they'd come out of a gumball machine. On her neck, starting below her ear and extending down into the mysterious unknown of her jacket, there was what looked to be a burn scar, the skin shiny and alien-looking.

"Yeah," Edmond said. "Just for the time being."

"It's not safe," she said. "But young people all think they're gonna live forever." Edmond wondered how old she was.

It was then that the waitress appeared, a genuinely young woman, probably still in high school. She hustled over to Edmond's table, hastily unwrapping a strip of lime green gum and popping it into her mouth, presumably to hide the cigarette smell.

"Sorry," she said, "I didn't see you come in."

"No worries," Edmond said. "What's the biggest plate I can get for seven—" no, tip, Edmond remembered, "—five dollars?"

The girl looked thoughtful for a moment. "You

like breakfast for dinner?" Edmond shrugged. "Okay, I'll bring you the Rise and Shine All-Day platter. That's got a lot of stuff."

"Thanks, miss," Edmond said. "And could I get some water as well?"

The girl nodded and scribbled something in her little notebook before heading over to the other booth. "Miss Chris, your roast beef sandwich is almost ready, you want some potatoes with that?"

"Girl, you gonna spoil me," the woman laughed. Her smile transformed her face into a moving tapestry of wrinkles.

"You . . . come through here a lot?" Edmond asked awkwardly. He couldn't imagine local people regularly patronizing this particular establishment.

"I got a class at the community college up here," the woman told him. "I go back and forth three times a week. Studying to be an ultrasound tech."

When he'd first seen her, Edmond had taken the woman for another traveler like himself, it surprised him a little to learn that she was rooted somewhere. "That's an interesting job," he said mildly.

"Not really," the woman answered, "but it's steady. Steady's good."

The waitress appeared again to set white ceramic cups of coffee before the two of them. "Oh no—" Edmond began, but she shushed him.

"I was finishing off the pot and you look like you need it anyways."

Edmond did need it. He hadn't even realized how hungry and how tired he was until that first hot gulp.

"She's a good girl," the woman said, wrapping her hands around the coffee cup to warm them.

Edmond made an agreeable noise in the back of his throat and sipped the coffee eagerly. He couldn't even tell if it was good coffee or not, it was just so satisfying to have something warm and familiar in his belly.

"I wish I had a friend like her when I was her

age. Woulda been good for me," the woman murmured, almost to herself.

Somewhere in the back, someone had turned on a radio, and, suddenly, music filtered out into the diner proper. The sound seemed to make the place cozier in a strange way, as though it shrank the cold, yellowish distance between everything.

"You headed anywhere in particular?" the woman asked.

"Just . . . California," Edmond said. It was probably stupid to head back to his home state but he couldn't think of anywhere else in the world to be. He no longer feared getting caught. He didn't fear much of anything, these days. The place inside him where he used to keep his anxieties was instead solid and inert, like a block of lead.

"Well congrats," the woman said wryly, "you made it."

"Yep," Edmond agreed. Outside, the sun was well and truly down now and the darkness was changing character from a deep navy blue to true black. He wondered where he was going to sleep—if he was going to sleep. Maybe he could talk the waitress into letting him crash in a booth? Probably not.

"It's getting harder to get around on foot these days," the woman said, as though she could read his thoughts. "All them automated cars. You don't got nothing they need."

"Yeah," Edmond said softly.

"I don't know that I'd trust it completely. Seems like it couldn't possibly make the kind of decisions a person can make on the fly like that. Judgments, I mean."

To this, Edmond had nothing to say.

"Back when I was hooking, a dude once picked me up in one of them. It's real interesting." She said it casually, almost fondly. Edmond opened his mouth to follow up on this admission but was interrupted by the waitress, who bore huge, steaming plates on her arms.

Edmond's meal did indeed come with "lots

of stuff"—baked beans, chunk-cut potatoes, sausage links, and, naturally, eggs—and he tucked in immediately, the other woman momentarily forgotten. The woman applied herself to her roast beef sandwich with similar intensity. "Enjoy!" the waitress told them cheerfully.

"So you . . . uh . . . traveled around a lot?" Edmond said, after clearing his plate and giving it a swipe with a piece of toast just to be sure. It had been about three days since he'd had a full meal. He'd been making do on granola bars and the occasional pack of convenience store jerky.

"When I was going solo," the woman said, "I spent a lot of time in places just like this." She gestured around them, encompassing not just the restaurant, but the larger building, the pay showers, the rows of oddments and energy drinks, the big diesel pumps outside. "I was never set up enough to get a real place. When I was real young, I worked in Cleveland, Ohio, but that was with a pimp."

Edmond laughed and immediately regretted

it. Laughing was probably rude, but the woman didn't seem to mind; she chuckled a bit as well. "I was just wondering," Edmond explained, "why Cleveland?"

"You mean the jewel of the Midwest?" the woman said, dry as a bone. "I was born there, it was my hometown. I didn't have to go too far to get in trouble. Hell, my first pimp was my daddy's brother."

"Fuck," Edmond muttered.

"Yep." The woman popped the last bit of sandwich into her mouth and chewed agreeably. "I was real young, though. I didn't realize what a shit deal it was until later. Went solo after I got this." She gestured to the scar on her neck. "I was sleeping— dope sick—when I shoulda been working, and my boyfriend woke me up with a pan full of boiling water. Could have killed me. I left as soon as I healed up."

"That's terrible." It sounded lame even in Edmond's own ears.

"It was, yeah," the woman admitted. "It got better, though. I just had to watch out for the johns, then." She shrugged, as though this were all in the most distant of pasts, scarred over as hard and fibrous as the burn marks on her skin. "I worked it until it didn't work no more. Now I do this. It's something steady and that's good for me."

Edmond turned to look at her, her drooping profile, a tiny head perched upon her massive winter coat. He realized now why the woman looked familiar to him: she was the girl in the newspaper, or she could have been. Rewind the years and the thousand little miseries, plump her face, apply a child's idea of womanly makeup and there she was. Alone and exploited.

"Would you trade it?" Edmond asked. The woman screwed up her forehead at him. "Would you trade your life for a better one, if it meant that someone else would live it in your place?"

There were bells over the door. Edmond noticed them for the first time now when they jangled as someone pushed their way in. It was a man with a baseball cap and some sort of uniform-type coveralls. He was carrying a large, cardboard box, hugged close to his chest like a child, and he stood just inside the doorway, fidgeting.

The woman heaved a mighty sigh and muttered, "Again?" under her breath.

The waitress, hearing the bells, came around the hostess stand wearing an uncomfortable, pasted-on smile. "Hey," she said, gentle and slightly reluctant, the way someone might talk to an overly affectionate aunt. "What's going on, Reggie?"

"Um. Elfie had her puppies. And I know that you said . . . You said she was cute. So I thought—" The way he spoke made him seem younger than he looked, or perhaps Edmond had just guessed wrong. He wouldn't look the waitress in the eye. He was trying to hide the way his hands were shaking, but the motion traveled through to the cardboard box, sending it trembling.

"Are there puppies in there?" The waitress' eyes

brightened, seemingly against her will. She stood up on her tiptoes to peer inside the box and the man didn't say anything, just beamed at her and tipped the box forward slightly.

"Awwwwwww." The sound drew out to a sharp little pinpoint and the waitress' hands vanished into the box only to emerge clutching a dark brown lump.

"Sheena!" It was a disembodied male voice, like Oz the Great and Powerful, from somewhere in the kitchen. "What the fuck? You can't have dogs in here."

"Jesus, all right!" the waitress—Sheena—snapped over her shoulder. She cradled the little pile of fur against her uniformed breasts. "C'mon." She jerked her head at Reggie. "Let's go outside for a sec."

Then, as though the thought had just occurred to her, she half-turned to look back at Edmond and the woman. "You all doin' okay?" Her face willed them to say "yes" and though the woman was clearly ready for the check and Edmond was hoping for another cup of coffee, they both nodded. The woman shooed her towards the door.

"Go on," she said.

The door twinkled closed behind them.

"You know that guy?" Edmond asked. The woman shook her head.

"Not really. In passing, I suppose. He lives up on the mountain with them weirdo cult people. He doesn't seem like a bad kid, but I don't like seeing Sheena mixed up with all that shit."

The woman rustled in her big coat, eventually pulling out a little clutch purse of the type that Edmond's mother would have called a "pocket-book." She counted out her bill; clearly she knew the amount from regular experience, then she stood up and adjusted her coat around her, tipping the hood back up over her face.

"I don't think it works that way," she said, pausing in front of his table and looking uncertain about it. Edmond looked up at her, bewildered. "Your question. I thought about it and I don't think it works that way. I think there's always more than enough shit to go around." She patted the table in front of him delicately, as though to emphasize her point. And then she was gone, just the strange, bundled shape of her pushing out the door and fading into the distant night.

Edmond sat with his mouth slightly open, unable to decide exactly what he wanted to say. All he could think was: *I wanted to save you.*

After a moment, he looked down at the table. The woman had slipped him a twenty, folded up twice and tucked underneath his plate.

---○---

Edmond left a big tip and Sheena beamed at him. It didn't feel right, asking about staying here for free. So, instead, he thanked her and told her to have a good night and walked out the front door with purpose, looking for all the world like someone with somewhere, anywhere, else to go.

He was surprised to find the young man, Reggie, standing outside. It had gotten colder since Edmond arrived and when Reggie blew into his hands, his breath was ghostly white.

"Oh, hey." Edmond sounded as though he had met a friend in an unexpected location. Reggie gave him a sideways look.

There was a little scratching, shifting sound, like something rubbing against cardboard. Edmond looked down at the box. "Isn't it a little cold for the—" He gestured at the box.

"I got a portable heat lamp on them," Reggie said. The man himself did not apparently warrant such consideration.

"You waiting on a lift?" Edmond asked. It was a long shot with the way that Reggie was looking at him, but he didn't think anyone else would be passing through tonight. It was either try to get a ride with Reggie or sleep rough somewhere around the truck stop itself.

"No," Reggie reacted as though Edmond had

hurled some vile accusation at him. "I have my bike." He'd biked here with the giant box, heat lamp and all? "I'm waiting for Sheena's shift to end."

"Does she . . . uh . . . know you're waiting?"

Reggie gave him such a furious look that, for a moment, Edmond was sure that the other man was about to fight him. "Yes! She wants a puppy. I'm waiting to give her one."

"Okay." Edmond tried to sound as inoffensive as possible. He leaned over to look inside the box. The puppies were nestled against one another, resting on a bed made of what looked like worn-thin kitchen towels. There was indeed a small yellow bulb illuminating their tiny snouts and squeezed-shut eyes. "Very . . . cute," Edmond said. He himself had never had pets and, if he did, he probably wouldn't have started with a dog. Cats were more suited to his lifestyle. Perhaps birds. Of course, there was no beast on earth suited to life as he was living it at the moment.

"They aren't supposed to be cute. They're supposed to be protection."

"Well, not for at least a few months," Edmond pointed out. Now he was just needling the boy. To be fair, Reggie was clearly profoundly needle-able.

"No, as soon as they're weaned they can smell one of those things and warn you."

"What things?" Edmond asked and Reggie seemed to realize immediately that he had said something wrong.

"Nothing." He looked off into the distance, as though expecting something of interest to wander by and change the conversation. There was, of course, nothing of interest around the truck stop.

"Do you mean like criminals and stuff?"

"Yeah," Reggie said, too quick and not remotely believable. He was an abysmal liar.

So Edmond tried a little awkward honesty of his own. "Is it for . . . evil spirits? Or something?" He gestured back towards the diner, still illuminated.

Sheena could be seen languidly bussing the remains of Edmond's dinner. "A woman in there said you were part of some cult around here?"

Reggie let out a snort of laughter. It was absurd, that sound of mirth coming from his seemingly perpetually angry face. "It's not a cult, she don't know what the fuck she was talking about."

"So what is it, then?"

"It's a community," Reggie said. He sounded like he was reading it off the back of a prescription bottle. "A community of like-minded people."

"Hmmm. That does kind of sound like the sort of thing someone in a cult might say . . . "

"We don't worship anything. It's not religious. We're just people who want to get away from . . . certain aspects of modern life. We live simple."

"Like the Amish," Edmond supplied.

Reggie glowered. "I said it's not religious. We just like to keep things human. Stay away from . . . that other stuff."

"Like . . . self-driving cars?" Edmond asked

slowly. Reggie made a noncommittal noise in the back of his throat.

"That's part of it," Reggie answered. "That's a symptom, though. The whole problem is too much automation. Machines doing things people are perfectly capable of doing. It's not . . . safe." Reggie breathed in deep through his nose. His slightly doughy face looked suddenly distant and superior. "People don't see that now but they'll find out the hard way. And we'll still be here. And we'll be prepared."

"That's . . . interesting." It was one of those moments that Edmond had experienced with greater regularity over the years: a real education about just how big his little project had grown. Now there were communities built around opposing his life's work?

And wouldn't that, in a weird way, make an excellent place for him to hide? No one was looking for a wanted roboticist amongst some neo-luddites fucking around in the woods. They probably assumed that he was still with . . . with Hart or her people or someone like them. They assumed he was holed up building more and more Bots by the day. Edmond almost laughed. No one had any idea just how useless he really was.

The lights in the diner went out all at once. Suddenly, they were cast all in shadows, the only glow coming from the little heat lamp in the box. Reggie looked ghostly, faintly yellow and flickering as he moved back and forth slightly, stamping his feet to keep them warm.

"She'll be out soon." Reggie spoke softly, reassuring Edmond. Edmond did not think he had asked for reassurance, but perhaps he had, if not in so many words.

At some point, the moon had risen over the horizon and it was bloated and white now, floating in the sky like a celestial larva. In the cardboard box, the little puppies jostled. Something had made them restless and they produced little squeaking yips of protest or excitement.

"Are they okay?" Edmond asked.

"Yeah. That's good. Means they're doing what's in their nature. That's what you want."

What else, Edmond thought, could anyone ask for?

THREE

ROOMMATE WANTED

Las Cuevas, CA. May, 2047

Shannon was absolutely not going to put someone on the lease just because he was incredibly, almost absurdly good looking.

She had told herself that no less than three times over the course of the weekend.

And yet, she kept reading and re-reading Archie's emails. There were only three, first the initial email where he was responding to her posting for a roommate. He included a few autobiographical details and offered to give references. Then a quick scheduling e-mail to find a mutually good time to meet and see the apartment. Finally a cordial one-liner, thanking her for showing him the apartment "no matter how it shakes out."

Fuck.

Shannon didn't have any particular expectations for Archie before he showed up—he was actually one of four people she was showing the apartment to that day. He was, admittedly, the only straight man on the list, but Shannon wasn't fazed by that. She'd lived with Felix, after all, for years, and neither of them had ever considered the other to be a viable sexual prospect. Which was perfect; it was virtually impossible to negotiate an even halfway fair utilities and groceries split with someone you were banging and Shannon had seen more than once the incredible fallout when a couple broke up but still had to share a living space.

Those were all really good reasons not to rent to someone she was attracted to. Super-good reasons.

Of course, just because she was attracted to someone didn't mean she was necessarily going to get embroiled in a relationship—sexual or otherwise—with them. She wasn't an animal, she could create and maintain boundaries. And Archie was the only person on the list who had a full-time job and real references, not just a ninth-grade English teacher or a best friend. Some might argue that choosing Archie would be the more mature thing to do.

Shannon had had only one steady boyfriend during her time in college. They dated through the second half of her freshman year and all of her sophomore year. She usually described their breakup as a "drifting apart," but the truth was, she eventually started to find his constant presence nettlesome rather than comforting.

After that, she dated casually and found that she reached what she thought of as her "saturation point" much more quickly. She had been forced to conclude that she didn't really like the idea of sharing her life so intimately with another person, though she occasionally found an individual compelling. In the end, Shannon herself was the only person whose company she could tolerate all the time, and even that was frequently painful.

Not that she was dating Archie. Or renting to him. Or doing anything at all with him. And so there was no reason to keep aimlessly floating between his last e-mail and the limited social media profiles she'd found for him.

She had done at least a cursory Googling for all of the roommate candidates, of course, but all of Archie's profile pictures were of inanimate objects, pets, or (presumably) himself as a child. He was a law student and a bartender, he was three years older than her, and he was committed to staying in the area for at least two more years, which was more than Shannon could say for herself.

She didn't know exactly what she had expected. "Law school" always conjured up two disparate images: bro-y guys floating merrily through their academic career, and second-generation strivers. Archie didn't seem to be either.

He was ten minutes late to their meeting and

interrupted her as she was microwaving popcorn. She answered the door while the bag was still revolving and both of them could smell the unmistakable burning, but neither of them said anything.

Archie was considerably taller than her, which was unusual. He had a "day-after" beard and dark, tightly-curled hair. His eyes were unusual, the color of amber when lit by the sun, and she noticed he had epicanthic folds, though his face did not strike her as particularly Asian.

Then he smiled at her and the microwave wailed and still Shannon did not speak. He looked as though he'd been carved rather than born. Carved out of some precious and remote wood, deep-grained and dark. He stuck out his hand and Shannon took it, still on autopilot.

"Shannon Liao?" he asked.

Shannon nodded like an idiot. His hand was warm and dry but not soft. It had all sorts of interesting planes and textures and she had the insane thought that she would like to spend hours mapping the topography of his skin.

"Hey," she managed finally. It sounded like someone was stepping on her throat.

And then the silence again.

"I'm Archie," he said finally. "From the . . . e-mail."

Shannon suddenly realized that she had been holding his hand (because she had ceased to shake it long ago) for roughly twenty seconds. That was such a long time to be holding a stranger's hand. She dropped it immediately and barely suppressed a little cry, as though she were shaking a poisonous bug off her skin.

Archie didn't seem to mind. He pursed his lips (*oh, God*) and rocked back on his heels slightly.

"Come in," Shannon said. Her voice sounded too loud to her, like a machine that had just kicked on in an empty room. "Come in and see the place."

She stepped back so he could get past her. As he went, she caught the faintest whisper of his scent—some soap she didn't recognize and the barest hint of sweat.

"It's two bedrooms," Shannon said, "obviously."

Archie peered around the living room, nodding approvingly at the sofa and the little parson's table, the small television, and the bar that demarcated the kitchen.

"Felix's stuff is still in his room, but you can get a feel for what the room is like normally. He'll definitely be moved out by the end of the month."

Archie opened and closed the closet and looked out the window, still silent. Shannon stood in the door behind him and twisted her hair around her finger. She wrapped and pulled her hair until it began to cut into the skin of her finger. The pain was fresh and immediate and brought her back to reality.

"It's . . . nice," Archie said, turning around to smile sheepishly at her, hands in both of his pockets. His voice was deep and pleasantly steady.

It was the kind of voice you'd want to talk you through an emergency landing.

"Yeah," she answered.

Again with the silence. And the staring. And the silent staring. She had to stop looking at his face. Also the rest of him. She had to say something. This was way too long to not have said something . . .

"The rent is eight-fifty per month. That includes utilities. It's a pretty good deal for the location. There's a laundry room in the activities center. Also there's an activities center. It's for . . . activities."

Oh, for fuck's sake.

"I don't go there much," Shannon added. "As you can tell."

To her relief, he laughed in a seemingly genuine way. Shannon reminded herself that she didn't have to impress him. If anything, he should be trying to impress her.

As if reading her mind, Archie spoke. "I'm gonna level with you. I like this place. It's a good location for me and it's in my price range. And you seem cool."

Shannon willed herself not to grin. She suppressed it, but just barely.

"I've got a steady work history and good rental references, if you want those. I don't smoke, or have pets, or wild parties. I'm a law student, so I'm pretty quiet. I do work nights on the weekends, though." The light from the window behind him outlined his silhouette, lean and appealing with a slight slouch that suggested easy confidence.

Shannon nodded as though taking this all in. In reality, she knew that she wouldn't be able to properly evaluate anything until he was no longer here, distracting her.

"That sounds great," she said. "I have a few other people to meet." She didn't, but Archie didn't need to know that. "So I'll let you know when I make my decision."

Archie smiled at her and there was something rueful in his face, as though he considered her decision a foregone conclusion. "Well, thanks for showing me the place."

"Thanks for . . . seeing the place." It sounded inane as she was saying it but, yet again, she couldn't seem to stop herself.

She guided him to the door and he extended his arm, probably to shake her hand again but, for one wild moment, she thought he was going to hug her. Shannon opened her arms automatically and then she saw the bewilderment in Archie's face and immediately realized her mistake. She dropped her arms just as Archie opened his and why didn't someone make and distribute portable trap doors that one could deploy at a moment's notice?

Uncertain, the two of them wound up sort of bumping their torsos together, arms firmly at their sides. It was like how Shannon imagined penguins would say goodbye to one another.

After he had gone, she retrieved her ruined popcorn from the microwave. Even the side of the bag was scorched black. Well, that made at least two minor disasters today.

Ever since then, she had been studiously not looking up Archie's details and definitely not trying-and-failing to discover whether or not he had a girlfriend. She had also been ignoring the increasingly discordant buzzes of her cell phone. Her father had stepped up his calling regimen and she still hadn't answered, though she couldn't say exactly why.

It frustrated her, how she heaped anxieties and neuroses on the smallest, most banal activities. Once, at the state fair, she had sat and watched the cotton candy man make each confection. He used a plain paper tube and pulled little wisps of colorful candy floss from the sides of a metal drum, gradually building a shape like an old fashioned beehive hairdo. Shannon sometimes felt as though her brain worked in that way: so much angst, but it was made of nothing in particular, just sugar and air and velocity.

Later. She would call her father later. Or maybe send him an e-mail. Somehow, typing a message seemed far less onerous than speaking on the phone. When she navigated back to her inbox, however, she was surprised to see a new email had apparently arrived in the thirty seconds she wasn't brooding over Archie's message.

The email address was strange; there was no website associated with it, just a name, *frederesse*, and the subject line was *see 4 urself*. Shannon's first thought that it was spam but that name was familiar to her. She stared at it for several moments before it dawned on her: someone using the same screen-name had uploaded that weird coffee shop video of the guy cutting himself.

After her failed search for any sort of independent corroboration, she had sent the uploader a message through the site's system: *Can I get a few more details? Would like to confirm or deny this one.*

That had been almost a week ago, though, and Shannon had all but forgotten about the incident, the way she often forgot about her minor obsessions. She hadn't messaged him from an account even remotely associated with Shannon Liao and now he had contacted her via her student e-mail. It certainly wasn't impossible to piece together Shannon's different usernames—she wasn't really trying to hide anything, after all—but it was a little creepy that this guy felt the need to do so. Was it supposed to be some kind of message, like, "I see you," or whatever?

Shannon wasn't going to be intimidated by some Internet rando. She tapped the e-mail and read it quickly; there wasn't much to read.

they r in all major cities

yours too

find the mod freaks they will know where 2 be

"What the fuck?" Shannon said aloud, though no one was around to witness her confusion. Shannon spoke six languages but apparently "Internet idiot" wasn't one of them. What the hell were "mod freaks"? Like, moderators? Modernists? British teenagers from the sixties?

She wasn't exactly shocked that her correspondent hadn't actually offered any verifiable details about the incident in the video. It was probably just another piece of Internet apocrypha, impossible to chase down because it was based on nothing at all.

It was then that her inbox gave a cheerful little *ding*. Another message, again from *frederesse*, this one containing only a link. It was a private blog, mostly in French, but Shannon was able to parse it. The blog's author was a student in Brussels, Belgium and they described a frightening scene shockingly similar to what Shannon had seen on the video. Apparently, it had gotten worse after the video cut out. The blogger said that the strange man had "peeled himself like a stewed tomato."

At the bottom of the post, there were a number of photos. Cell phone pictures, but pretty clear ones. They showed the interior of the café in the video, this time from several different angles; Shannon could see the gathered crowd (the filmmaker probably amongst them) and the last photo included the man. His face was a ruin of red, blood, and tissue alike. It was hard to tell because he had clearly been moving, fighting against the two other men who were attempting to restrain him, but Shannon could see a pale, blurry flap of what she presumed to be his facial skin.

"Ugh." Shannon grimaced and snapped the link closed. Well, it wasn't a newspaper but it wasn't nothing, either. At least two people had witnessed this . . . whatever it was. And at least one of them was able to nail it down to a specific café in Brussels in the summer of '45.

Of course, even if it *had* happened exactly the way the video showed, that didn't mean that this guy was some . . . ultra-realistic robot that was just running around on the loose. People performed incredible physical feats all the time. It was entirely possible that an insane person could mutilate themselves.

Some people had incredible pain tolerances. Gia, the tattoo artist at the studio where Shannon had gotten her heartbeat implants, for example; she'd had all her fingers surgically broken and stretched to make them eerily long and graceful.

Oh shit, Shannon thought, *that's what he meant!* Mod freaks. *Body* modification freaks. It made a kind of sense; if there really were hyper-realistic Bots, people like Gia would be first in line to check out their hardware and—

If Shannon was still seeing her therapist, the woman would have known exactly what she was doing right now. She called it "avoidance," when Shannon sank herself into an unrelated task to stave off doing something more difficult. In this case, it was graduation, her father, the next step, which had quickly become more of a leap. Shannon didn't want to deal with those things so she was digging into this dumb Bot thing and fawning over Archie. Her therapist would also have said that she needed to learn how to prioritize and how to shift out of negative behavior patterns, but Shannon quit seeing her therapist two years ago.

It couldn't hurt to stop in and say "hi" to Gia and to feel her out a bit. It couldn't hurt to wait another day before deciding about the apartment. To assuage her guilt, Shannon picked up the phone and scrolled through her contacts.

Her father answered on the third ring.

FOUR

COMMUNE

Edmond knew that he was drifting. He was just waiting for something, anything, to snag upon and hold him still. If it wasn't a cult of quasi-luddites in the Northern California woods, it would be something else. Or maybe he would just go until he stopped. Maybe he'd just float out into the ocean and be done with it?

There was no easy way into what Edmond was already calling "the compound" in his head. He'd hitched a ride up the interstate, but had gotten out at the 19 mile marker, as he'd been instructed. The way in was a narrow, twisty road, little more than a slight gap between the trees. Edmond walked a half-mile past it before realizing he'd missed it. He wondered what the road could possibly have been for. It seemed too small even for a logging or fire road.

It was a six and a half mile walk. He'd been warned about that. Edmond considered himself lucky to have gotten a lift as far as he did.

It did feel a little primeval, the glistening jade of the leaves and the incredible deadened stillness all around him. Edmond wasn't exactly an "outdoorsy type" but he could see how this sort of place could appeal to a troubled soul.

And Edmond was that.

Reggie had told him (in a hilariously reluctant tone) that everyone was welcome up at the "community" but that anyone who wanted to stay there had to pull their own weight while they did so. Edmond liked the idea of that, of being useful once again. He had been so inert for so long—or rather, he had made himself inert. He felt like a late-stage

King Midas, shut up in his palace, refusing to touch anything for fear of destroying it entirely.

The dog was an unusual deep brown color, and it blended in so fully with the trees and their shadows that Edmond didn't even notice it at first. It was only when the animal moved its head to follow his progress that Edmond saw the creature.

Edmond had a stupid thought: *Is that a wild dog?* It was well-fed, sleek-coated. It was a domesticated animal, though it didn't wear a collar or a harness. It was still looking at him, just watching him as though supervising his trip through the woods.

Edmond rifled in his jacket pockets, eventually producing the dried and brittle end of a jerky stick. He lowered himself into a crouch and stretched out his hand, jerky in his palm. The dog's wet black nose wriggled slightly and it took an uncertain step forward. Edmond waited, making himself as still as he could be.

Eventually the dog loped up to him, eagerly snuffling the dried meat from his palm. When the jerky was gone, the dog assiduously licked his skin clean of any remaining particles. Edmond withdrew his hand and patted his head, as much to get rid of the dog-slime as to ingratiate himself with the animal.

The dog looked up at him, a steady but not unfriendly gaze. Then the animal turned and trotted off down the road towards, presumably, Edmond's destination. After a moment, he followed the beast.

It reminded him unavoidably of the illicit weed farm where he and Hart had laid low in those first heady days after they had fled the lab. That place was crawling with dogs as well.

"They're the best security system you can get," Little Rick had told him once. "Sometimes the low-tech way is the best way."

The dogs never liked Hart. Though she regularly made awkward overtures to them with handfuls of kibble or even bits of raw meat, they would not approach her and they wouldn't eat anything she had touched. Not even if she dropped it to the ground. They eventually stopped barking whenever they saw her but they never lost that still wariness, a stiffness in their whole body as though, at any moment, they might need to attack.

———o———

The community had no fences or walls or doors to bar entry. It was an open-ish space in the middle of the forest, though Edmond could see the remnants of ground-down stumps where someone had felled trees to make space. There were a series of houses that were not exactly houses, more like "dwellings" than anything else.

Edmond recognized some of the buildings as yurts, constructed with the inexpensive kits that people could buy online. They were large, one-room buildings, circular in shape with a peaked roof. There were perhaps half a dozen of them and someone had put down walkways of wooden planks to go between them.

There were other, less uniform buildings as well. One metal box that looked suspiciously like a cargo container, a couple of actual trailer homes and some minuscule boxy structures that looked as though they had been built on-site.

It was approaching nightfall when Edmond arrived and the deep forest only accelerated the oncoming dark. Yet some of the houses produced an ailing yellow glow and there were white Christmas lights strung up between the houses to illuminate the walkways. So they didn't eschew *all* the trappings of modern life, then. They also must have had a generator somewhere up here; Edmond highly doubted that they were on the local power grid.

It wasn't until Edmond and his canine guide cleared the tree line that he heard the other dogs, yipping and howling and offering deep, chesty "woofs" from inside the DIY houses. There must have been more than a dozen of them. It was like a neighborhood of dogs crammed into one smallish clearing.

Then came the other noises, more human sounds of stirring and investigation. Edmond heard murmurs and rustles and, slowly, shadowy shapes began to emerge from the buildings. Some of the dogs squeezed out around them and made their way over to Edmond. One, with long, curled ears danced in front of Edmond merrily, barking a warning or a greeting. It was hard to tell with dogs.

"Brandy, leave it!" said a woman's voice from the darkness. She pushed aside the flimsy bamboo-style door of a nearby yurt and emerged, wild-haired and disgruntled. She had another dog at her side, twin to the one that had led Edmond here. His dog, in fact, defected as soon as he saw the woman and ran over to her side.

As the woman approached Edmond, some of the others hung back. It looked like mostly men to Edmond, but perhaps only men came to inspect newcomers. Edmond stepped forward into the glow of the Christmas lights and tried to look non-threatening.

The woman was small—a head and a half smaller than him—but business-like. Her hair was a mass of fat and shiny black curls. Edmond wondered idly how she managed to keep her hair so frizz-free out here in the middle of nowhere. She was wearing a denim work shirt, dirty jeans, and hiking boots. She was frowning at him.

"You the hitchhiker?" she asked.

Edmond nodded. "I guess so."

"Reggie said you would be coming. We assumed you'd come during business hours."

Edmond resisted the urge to laugh. Business hours? What was this, a hedge fund? What "business" did they do up here in the hills?

"Sorry," he said instead, "I miscalculated a little bit."

She sniffed and dug into her pants pocket, producing the crumbled remains of a milk bone, which she distributed to the now three dogs flanking her.

"Go lay down," she said, pointing at the open yurt behind her. They all obeyed, except for the dog who had guided Edmond. The animal lingered, looking back at the woman with pitiful eyes.

"And you, Brandy," she said, pointing again. Finally, the dog turned and vanished into the dwelling.

The woman faced Edmond again. She scrutinized his face in the limited light from the overhead bulbs. "Well," she said, "the dogs didn't alert on you."

"That's . . . good?"

The woman sighed and looked over her shoulder. For the first time, he noticed the others lingering around the buildings and, presumably, watching them warily. "I've got this one," she called out. "He's okay."

"Here," she reached out and took Edmond's hand. He could feel a hard, raised scar over the backs of her knuckles. She pulled him towards the yurt while he watched the other figures melt back into the gloaming.

Edmond had to admit, the interior of the yurt was surprisingly spacious. The woman had strung a hammock bed across the upper reaches of the room and the entire circumference was free for habitation.

"Good use of space," Edmond said, gesturing towards the open floor, covered in a worn, multi-colored carpet.

"Thanks." The woman hovered over what appeared to be a little hot plate. There was a glass pan full of water on top of it, just starting to bubble. "You want coffee or anything?"

Edmond shook his head. He had spent so much time recently going without regular meals that the gnawing in his belly had almost ceased to be a misery. It was more like an old injury he had learned to accommodate.

The woman left the hot plate and pulled what looked like a cushion for lawn furniture out from the edge of the room. She offered one to Edmond and the two of them sat on the floor, facing one another. "I'm Sylvie Solis," she said, extending her hand for shaking. Edmond did so dutifully.

Sylvie Solis stared at him and it occurred to Edmond that she was waiting for him to introduce himself. If he were really a smart man and not simply a man convinced that he was smart, he would have developed a cover story and fake name before this precise moment. Instead, he hadn't even thought about what he was going to tell people. All he'd thought about was finding a place to land, at least for a little while.

If Sylvie and her group were following Bot development at all, they probably knew his name and there was no way they would allow him into their midst. "I'm . . . Eddie," Edmond offered eventually. Not his most inspired moment but it would, at least, be easy to remember. "Eddie Graves." It was his mother's maiden name. If anyone did even a cursory web search on Edmond West that would discover his subterfuge immediately. Luckily, he was surrounded by the people least likely in all the world to ever do a web search for anything.

"Nice to meet you, Eddie," Sylvie said. "What brings you to us tonight?"

Yet another question that Edmond couldn't answer in a remotely credible way. "Well, I met your guy, Reggie, at the truck stop . . . "

Sylvie smiled. She had a nice smile, plump pink lips and large white teeth. Her smile made the flesh dimple just on the right side of her face. She looked very healthy and scrubbed, like a poster girl for some product with a lot of "natural ingredients." "Yeah," she said, "our friendship ambassador. Sorry if he was rude to you."

"No, no, he was fine. He told me about this place and I thought . . . " Yes, what had Edmond thought? " . . . I didn't have anywhere else to go, honestly." He was being honest; Edmond West had reached the end of the world, as far as he was concerned. He had once heard—or more likely read—that the best lies contained some small element of truth. Perhaps that was why Sylvie's face seemed to soften as he spoke.

"You're not the first person to tell me that," she assured him.

"How, uh, how long have you been . . . doing this?"

Sylvie raised her eyebrows. "Me personally?" Edmond had taken her for the leader of this little commune, but apparently she too had come here from somewhere else. "About a year and a half. I was working as a forest ranger in the area and Herbie came to me when he was starting this place up, said he needed someone who knew the woods."

"Herbie?"

"Herbie's the idea man. He's the one who came up with the concept of a place where people could prepare for the problems of the future. There were a lot of us worried about the direction the country's going in, but we were all spread out, all living solo.

Herbie brought us together because he knew that a community is stronger than any one individual."

It was probably this sort of speech that had people thinking Sylvie and her folks were cultists.

"He's also the money-man." Sylvie grinned her dimpled grin. "His family used to own most of the land around here. Lumber-barons. This five hundred fifty-acre parcel is the last of their holdings and he gifted it to the community in perpetuity."

"That's . . . nice of him."

"Not nice. Just practical. Herbie can see what's coming, just like the rest of us. He's doing what he can to get us safe through to the other side. We need more people like him."

Edmond nodded and remained silent, the very same way he would if a nice old lady at the grocery store started talking to him about Jesus.

"You can be straight with me, if you just need some food and a place to crash for a few days, we can do that for you," Sylvie offered. "You wouldn't be the first person to try out this life and say 'Hey, maybe this isn't for me.' We live simple up here and it's hard, but we think it will eventually be much harder the other way."

"I don't know about . . . all that stuff," Edmond told her. "About robots and . . . things. But I like simple. I haven't had simple in a very long time." The truth of it surprised Edmond even as he spoke. His life had gotten unbearably complex and he longed for the ease of a single compulsion, a life composed nearly exclusively of work.

Sylvie slapped the carpet on either side of her knees. "Well, okay then! You can sleep with Miguel and Stevie tonight and then in the morning, we'll see about fitting you in around here."

Edmond gave her a grin. It wasn't as nice as her own, but it was all he had. "Thank you," he said, "I would really like that." She looked like she believed him which was just right because the best lies have a little bit of truth in them after all.

—o—

Daylight did no favors for the little settlement. The buildings looked dumpier, the construction flimsier. Even the lights seemed like especially limp, black threads outlined against the blue sky. There were several muddy little gardens and other spots where the earth was tilled and ready for planting. There were a number of small green plants springing up, mostly unblossomed.

He found the generators as well, four of them, clustered together like old metal filing cabinets. Only one of the generators was on, and there were several red plastic cans of fuel stacked around their bases.

There was also a well covered with a weathered wooden pallet. A slender water pipe and spigot emerged from the pallet with a heavy red handle. A coil of green hose was heaped next to it and someone had packed straw all around the area, presumably to insulate the pipe during the colder months.

Next to the pump handle and apparently

growing wild was a single Bird of Paradise. It jutted out nearly sideways from the earth, the long, beak-like bloom sipping at the ground much like a real bird might do. Edmond crouched down beside the flower and touched it, gentle so as not to actually disturb the plant. He was surprised to see it here; they liked the warmer weather and lots of sunshine. He wondered if someone had been so foolishly optimistic as to plant it here in the middle of the forest or if a rogue pollen spore had made a particularly unlikely journey.

"It's broke," the voice behind him was high and grating. A child.

"The flower?"

The child—it was a girl—drew up beside him. "That's a flower?"

Edmond nodded. "It's called a Bird of Paradise."

The little girl took this in, appraising the purple curled leaves, the slender points of the orange petals. "What does it make?"

Edmond turned to look at her. She was maybe

seven or eight, her blonde hair in a high ponytail. She was wearing hiking boots, just like Sylvie. "It doesn't make anything," Edmond said. "It's just pretty."

The girl made a face, as though she'd tasted something sour. "Are you here to fix the water?"

Edmond was about to tell her "no," but he stopped himself. What *was* he here for, after all? "What's wrong with it?" he asked. The girl shrugged.

"No more water."

"Okay," Edmond said, "do you have any tools?"

The girl nodded and immediately ran off, presumably to fetch the aforementioned tools.

Edmond lifted the wooden pallet off the pump and set it aside carefully. He didn't want to crush the bird of paradise, not after it had overcome so much to bloom here in this inhospitable ground.

———O———

That was how Sylvie found the two of them later, Edmond half-buried in the top of the well, the pump's motor spread out in pieces on the grass beside him. The little girl crouched protectively over the pieces, arranging them neatly from small-est to largest.

"What are you doing?"

"Fixing the water," the girl chirruped.

Sylvie squatted down beside Edmond. She tilted her head until she could see him, fiddling in the bowels of the well. She laughed. It was a surpris-ingly deep sound for such a little woman. "Already on the job, eh?"

Edmond paused and adjusted his socket wrench against a bolt before looking up to face her. "No time like the present," he said.

"I admire your work ethic but you might be bark-ing up the wrong tree here. That motor's burned out. We're going to have to get a replacement."

Edmond nodded and picked up his wrench

again. "Probably," he said. "I'd just like to try something."

"You good with machines?" Sylvie asked, and there was nothing suspicious in her tone but still the question pulled Edmond up short. He stared down at the guts of the motor, spread before him like a heart patient's open chest.

"I just think sometimes people give up on things too quickly," he said, still not looking at Sylvie.

She didn't say anything, just hung over him, her long curly hair flopping down, almost skimming the top of his head. He could smell her; her hair at least. It seemed . . . deep and powdery, a little medicinal with a floral overlay. He liked it.

"Suit yourself, then," she said, still cheerful. "We got breakfast when you get done."

Sylvie rose and took the scent of her hair with her. Edmond didn't watch her leave. Instead, he beckoned the little girl closer. "Look at this," he said, pointing at the exposed motor. "Do you know how this works?"

The girl shook her head, grave and silent. She held a single screwdriver in her hands like a prayer candle. "All right," Edmond said, "pay attention and I'll show you."

It hadn't occurred to him until he invited the girl to look at the motor, but Edmond suddenly realized that he had done this, or something like it, once before. It was winter then, an unusually cold one, and he was ten years old. His father had not insulated the pipes in their own well properly and the unexpected cold snap had frozen them and utterly stopped the flow of water between the well and the house.

His father, wrathfully sober, had ringed the well with portable heaters, even dragged Wynette's hair-dryer out there, trailing an orange extension cord. His hands were red and clumsy with cold. Edmond held a huge flashlight on him and tried not to shiver. In the house, Wynette stood in front of the kitchen sink and awaited further instruction.

His father had not been able to fix the pipes,

but pipes were simple machines. They couriered water from one place to another and they were either cracked or whole, there was no wiggle-room. A motor was infinitely more complex than a pipe. And Edmond knew from experience that, as you increased the complexity of a machine, you increased the endless opportunities for change, transformation and, most importantly, new solutions to the oldest problems.

The little girl laughed when water burbled from the spout and stuck her hands in front of the flow, though it was cold enough to turn her skin bone white and then an irritated pink. Edmond joined her, rinsing the grease and dirt off his hands.

"Okay," he said, pushing the pump's handle off after a few moments. "Don't waste it."

The little girl eyed the pump. She reached out

and touched the pipe, just with two fingers. "It's gonna keep working?"

Edmond pulled the handle up abruptly, a burble of water escaped, splashing her hand and arm. The little girl laughed and Edmond shoved the handle down for good this time. "Yes," he said, "it's going to keep working now. And if it stops, we'll fix it again."

The little girl wiped her hand clumsily on her shirtfront and crouched down to pick up the tools and miscellaneous parts that Edmond had left scattered around the well's edge. They had surely missed the breakfast that Sylvie mentioned, but Edmond was hopeful that he might be able to prevail upon her hospitality once again. To that end, he set off for the yurt he had identified as Sylvie's. It was past noon now and several other people were out and about, most of them working in the little gardens, but there were also some other children playing in small groups. Almost every group had at least one dog with them, a lazing, floppy-tongued sentinel.

The people looked at him as he passed, but no one called out to him. Edmond supposed that new faces couldn't be too uncommon around the place. If people really did just pass through for a few days as Sylvie had suggested, maybe the other residents didn't bother getting to know everyone.

"Sylvie?" Edmond knocked on the door of her yurt, though it could hardly be called "knocking." Instead of a rapping sound, his knuckles merely shook the flexible wood of the door.

"C'mon in," Sylvie called out, "I'm just doing paperwork."

It was that little bit of extra information—information that he hadn't asked for—that might have tipped him off, if he were being careful. But he wasn't being careful, not since he left Hart behind. What else did he have left to protect?

He had just entered the yurt when someone hit him. He didn't know who it was; his eyes had not even had time to adjust from the transition to the indoors. The blow registered initially not as pain but as light—perfectly white and almost pretty. It blotted out his vision. He hit his knees and then the floor in quick succession. The light faded, leaving an afterimage of orange. After that, he knew no more.

FIVE

DIVES

If Shannon were being really, truly, completely honest with herself, Gia's hands did gross her out a little. Gia had told her that the doctors suggested she get skin removed from her thigh to cover her new, elongated fingers more fully, but she had resisted. "I don't want a scar on my ass," she said.

Privately, Shannon thought she definitely should have gone for the scar. Almost twice as much finger and half as much skin; it made her hands look all *Danse Macabre*. Shannon always had to studiously stop herself from staring.

"So, kiddo,"—Gia called everyone "kiddo"—"how are the LED dermals holding up?"

Shannon's hand drifted absently up to her chest. Sometimes she forgot they were there. At least until night came and they emitted their familiar, regular glow. Something of her mother, as close to her heart as possible. "They're great," she said.

"No infections or anything?" Gia unbuttoned the top of Shannon's shirt and peered at the little studs with a doctor's authoritative disinterest.

"Nope," Shannon smiled, "I've been using the special soap."

Gia smiled in return. Her left canine had been scored, carved like an old-fashioned ivory ornament. It featured a fierce mermaid, trident clutched in one fist. The work was incredibly tiny and detailed. You had to be really close to even notice it. "Good girl," Gia told her. "So what you got going on today? You looking for more work?"

Shannon did up her buttons. "Maybe," she said, "it kinda depends."

"You thinking something old-school? Are we finally gonna get some ink on you?" she nudged

Shannon in the ribs and wheeled herself over to the counter where they kept the art book.

"Oh God, my dad barely tolerates the dermals. A tat . . . yeah, I'd never stop hearing about that."

Gia handed her the book. It was heavy and wide, like a hair salon's style book. "It ain't his skin, kiddo."

Shannon had a feeling that, if Gia were to raise that objection with her father, he would disagree. He would say that he made every part of Shannon, skin and bones and everything in between. He would say that she didn't have anything that didn't come from him and from Shannon's mother. And now there was just him.

Shannon turned the pages slowly. She wasn't particularly drawn to tattoos herself, but she still liked to look at them. Here was a slightly trashy-looking fairy. Or "faerie" as the text indicated. Four pages of tigers, with a few other big cats sneaking in. A sheet of Chinese characters. Shannon rolled her eyes. "People still get these?"

"Oh come on," Gia said. "If we didn't have 'em, the drunk white girls would riot."

"That one's wrong," Shannon said, pointing at a character mid-way down the page. "It means strength but, like . . . tensile strength, I guess? Not emotional. That's not what they want."

Gia smiled at her like she was an adorable child. "I can tell you right now, they do not care."

"Also this one is upside down."

"Did you come here to proofread my art book?"

"Hey, correct translations are my business." Shannon was stalling. Gia could see it. "Actually, I came here because I wanted to ask you about some . . . more extreme stuff?"

Gia raised her painted-on eyebrows. "What did you have in mind?"

"I heard . . . from a friend that people were getting into some . . . mechanical stuff."

Gia just looked at her. She had a studied blankness to her, as though she were taking all of her cues from Shannon herself.

"I just heard that people were basing mods on things they saw with . . . um . . . with the Bots." She didn't specify the SennTech Bots. Gia breathed in deeply through her nose.

"That's a big leap, kiddo." Her voice had changed entirely, all the teasing had gone out of it and she was speaking in a near-whisper now. "You get one little thing done and you want to jump right to . . . structural changes."

"I don't want anything in particular right now," Shannon assured her, though she didn't know if that was actually true. She had put a lot of effort into this for someone who didn't want anything out of it. "I just want to know if it's possible."

"Well, I can tell you right now that it's possible. It's pretty extreme, though. Not something I'd think you'd go for. That's the kind of stuff you can't hide with a big sweater, you know?"

Shannon's gaze flickered down to Gia's, spindly fingers, splayed across her thighs like ghost-white spiders. "Have you gotten anything done?"

"No and I don't plan to. But I know some people . . . "

Shannon leaned forward and lowered her own voice. "Yeah?"

"It wasn't about cosmetics. Mostly. They wanted to . . . enhance some stuff. I don't know. It's not really my scene. It feels more like plastic surgery than body mod to me." She smiled at Shannon and, for the first time, it looked forced. "You're perfect already, what do you want with all that?"

"Gia, you know it's not about that. I just want some more information."

Gia heaved a great sigh and grabbed the art book from Shannon. "Okay, if you're dead set on it, I know a person who can tell you more about it. You know that none of this is exactly street legal, right? Like, if they catch you with this hardware inside your body, I'm not sure what would happen."

Shannon wasn't sure either. She had avoided thinking about robots until she found them sprouting up regularly in her school life. She considered that part of her father's world, and they were both happier when she had no idea what he did for work.

"Yeah," she said, "I can be discreet."

"You know The Grouper?"

Shannon couldn't suppress a little laugh. Everyone on campus knew The Grouper, the premiere drinking establishment for kids with shaky fake IDs, EverClear enthusiasts, and people looking to have sex and vomit in the same bathroom stall. Often at the same time.

"Uh, yeah," she said. She'd gone a few times in freshman year, like most people did. Once she turned twenty-one, there were approximately one billion better places to booze it up. Most of those other places didn't even have a semi-nude drunk guy lying in front of the jukebox and charging a toll.

"Well, he hangs out there most nights after midnight. If you tell him that you know me, he might talk to you."

That didn't sound extremely promising. "What's he look like?"

Gia pulled a face. "I could describe him, but he'd just sound like any other guy. But I think you'll know him when you see him."

"He isn't the guy who lies in front of the jukebox with his pants around his knees, is he?"

For the first time since she had brought up the issue of Bot modifications, Gia genuinely smiled before letting out one of her crazy, witch-cackle laughs. "Naw," she said, "not that guy."

Her face settled again into as much gravity as she could manage. "You'll find him," she said, "or he'll find you. One way or another."

---○---

What to wear to The Grouper? Shannon hadn't thought that particular thought in quite a while. Eventually, she decided on denim leggings and a tank top with a scoop neck. The neck dipped deep below her collarbones, exposing the LED lights embedded in her skin. She often wore clothing that hid her dermals, though not necessarily on purpose. Tonight, however, it felt best to show them. She had an idea that they might serve as a kind of badge of kinship, a membership card to the club of people who cut and re-arranged their bodies to suit their purposes.

The Grouper was at the end of a long street full of other student bars. The sports bar where the waitresses wore little shorts and the shouting spilled out into the streets, the rooftop bar that just served vodka and vodka-cocktails, a comfortable Western-themed bar where everyone had to sit on hay bales. And then there was The Grouper.

It was actually below street level and the entrance was just a series of stone steps, painted bluish-gray, and descending towards a single metal door embedded in the earth. It felt like walking into a bomb shelter. There was no bouncer at the door—the idea of a cover charge was patently absurd—and

Shannon just walked in, shutting the door politely behind her.

It was 12:10 (Shannon had always believed in the importance of punctuality) and the place was surprisingly full. A group of students, most assuredly freshman, if not students from a local high school, were posted up at a table in the back. All the better to hide their youthful faces in shadow.

The real dedicated drinkers were lined up at the bar. Someone had removed the jukebox—and the pantsless man with it. In its place was a pool table. The green felt was ripped and rumpled in several places and one of the sticks had a knot of tape wrapped around the middle, as though it had been broken and clumsily repaired.

The air was rich with a urine-y, mildew smell and Shannon watched herself enter via a huge mirror behind the bar. She looked anxious and she tried to stifle her expression, to make herself as blank as possible.

Shannon felt that she could safely dismiss the

table in the back. This man whom she would know on sight would not be a student. So she approached the bar and settled herself on one of the two free stools. She realized for the first time that she was the only woman in the room.

She used the bar mirror to examine each of the men seated in a row next to her. A mid-twenties guy with the look of a failed student athlete about him, definitely not on his first tumbler of bourbon. Next to him was a forty-something with a glass of beer, sipping slowly to stave off that terrible moment when he had to walk back up those stairs and go back to his real life. The third man was turned away from her, avidly watching the tiny, soundless TV in the corner. The channel was inexplicably tuned to some sort of Bollywood movie or music video. A beautiful woman winked at the camera as her hair fluttered in the wind. This wind was expected—even demanded—and she turned into it and closed her eyes, red mouth open in song.

That, Shannon decided, must be the guy. His

head was tilted too far back for her to really see his face but process of elimination suggested he had to be the person she was looking for.

"What can I get you?"

Shannon registered the voice as familiar before she even turned to look. The bartender was half-bent over an open trough of ice, and the dim light hit upon the edge of his jaw, making it look even more appealingly angular. Archie.

"This is where you bartend?" It came out sounding a lot angrier than Shannon had intended, as though she were accusing him of some nefarious business.

Archie didn't seem offended, though. When he looked up at her, he smiled. "Hey, it's Apartment Shannon."

"Shirley Temple."

Archie's forehead wrinkled up. "Shirley Temple Shannon?"

"No. That's what you can get me. A Shirley Temple."

It was hard to tell in the dingy dim and with Archie's dark skin, but Shannon thought she saw the smallest blush rise in his cheeks. "Oh. Yeah. Of course."

She watched the minute movements of his hands as he measured out the grenadine and sprayed a jet of soda water into the glass. He gave her extra cherries.

"Thanks," she murmured when he slid the glass towards her.

"Of course." He handed her a white napkin square. Shannon sipped her drink to avoid having to say anything. It was very sweet, but Shirley Temples always were. Shannon didn't know exactly why she ordered it, it was a tween girl's drink. Something about Archie made her incapable of critical thinking. "Yeah, I've worked here for about a year," Archie said. "The tips are shockingly good."

Shannon raised her eyebrow at him. "I'll take your word on that one."

"So, uh, what brings you here?"

There was no way in hell Shannon was going to answer that question. She also wanted to steer him away from questions about the apartment, which she had not seriously thought about in days. "Just . . . hanging out."

Archie's face was eager and open. He was about to say something when the gaggle of teenagers from the table appeared at the edge of the bar, requesting refills. Shannon had never been more thankful for a group of nineteen-year-olds loudly posturing. She took the opportunity to slide away from the bar and over to the man on the end, who was still watching the television.

Gia was right. Up close, there was something . . . different about him. Shannon might even say that something was "wrong," though what, precisely, that something might be, she couldn't say. She tapped him on the shoulder and he turned, offering her the very same smile he had aimed at the television.

"I'm a friend of Gia's," Shannon said.

His smile did not dim or change. When his hand reached out to clutch Shannon's own, she could imagine that the limb was operating entirely of its own accord. "C'mon," he said, pulling her by the hand towards the bathroom in the back.

Shannon glanced back at Archie as she went. He was occupied with the group, serving up their margaritas and mid-range beers. As the bathroom door swung shut behind her, she thought she saw him look up in her direction, but perhaps she only imagined it.

The bathroom was inarguably the worst part of The Grouper. It was unisex and only one of the stalls still had a door. Uninspired graffiti and band stickers covered every inch of the walls and people had even scrawled over the mirror. She had never known the faucets to function properly.

The strange man didn't seem bothered by the surroundings, however. He took a seat on the toilet in one of the open stalls. "Uh . . . are you sure you want to do that?" Shannon asked. He looked at her, genuinely bewildered.

"Why not?"

Shannon shook her head. "Nothing, nothing."

"So, Gia sent you?"

"Not exactly. I wanted to come for . . . myself. I wanted to ask you about mods. About Bots."

The man on the toilet seat nodded with the eager sunniness of a junior executive. "Okay, what do you want to know?"

Shannon started slightly. It seemed as though there should be more . . . pageantry. Code words, secret handshakes, that sort of thing. He seemed unnervingly comfortable with Shannon, a stranger to him.

He seemed to have noticed her hesitation because he stretched out both of his arms, as though inviting her for a hug. "Don't be scared," he said. "There's no reason to be scared."

"I'm not scared."

He shrugged. His arms were still stretched out,

though Shannon hadn't moved an inch. "Then talk to me." He sounded almost pleading and Shannon obliged him.

"What did you get done?"

"Oh, lots of things. First, my eyes." He reached up to his left eye and pulled the lower lid down grotesquely. Shannon, who had limited experience with the inside of the human eyelid, couldn't see anything wrong with it. "I was severely near-sighted for most of my life. Now I'm not. Now I see perfectly."

This sounded less like a robot-enabled miracle and more like quality eye surgery, but Shannon knew better than to bring that up.

"And I haven't slept in seven months," the man added. He didn't sound nearly so impressed with this change though it was by far the more interesting idea.

"How did you do that?"

He stabbed a finger at her and grinned a cheesy grin. "How do I *not* do it, don't you mean?"

Shannon stifled a sigh. "Yeah. Whatever. That."

"I got a total reconfiguration up there. They'll tweak anything you want. It looks insane," he tapped the side of his skull and did it make a slightly odd noise? Something other than the dense "thunk" Shannon was expecting?

"It *looks* insane?"

The man moved with a childlike eagerness, as though he had been waiting all night—maybe all his life—for someone to only ask him this very question. He dug his hands into his slightly shaggy brown hair and then, to Shannon's great surprise, he lifted his hair entirely off his head in one continuous piece.

"I had to get this stupid thing but pretty soon they'll legalize it and then I can get rid of it—"

He was saying something else, but Shannon wasn't listening. Her breath was locked in her throat. Her feet moved themselves forward until she was packed sardine-tight between the man and the wall of the bathroom stall. The entire back of his head was . . . not gone, exactly, but made translucent. Instead of skin or even white bone, he had something that looked like a fucked up aquarium window. Shannon touched it with two fingers, it felt utterly smooth, like the finest glass in the world. She withdrew her hands and tilted her head to see if she had left smudges on the surface.

But the real show was, as usual, underneath.

The man's brain was grayish-white. It looked dense and strong, like a clenched muscle. It had been fitted with . . . things. Wires, maybe? They looked like threads of dark hair and they skated over the rumpled surface of his brain, sinking down into the tissue here and there.

"Watch this," the man said. He made no visible movements, but suddenly a jet of blue light traced along one of those wires and vanished again, generated by his body and enclosed by it.

None of this seemed to cause him any pain though, obviously, it should have killed him. People couldn't just stick things in their brains.

They couldn't just replace half their skull with . . . some kind of weird plexiglass? This was well beyond anything Shannon had ever heard about and he had presumably gotten all this done on the down-low, not in some cutting-edge medical facility.

"Isn't it beautiful?" the man asked. "I never thought of the brain as a beautiful body part . . . That's what this has taught me. Everything inside of us is beautiful."

Usually, Shannon got a build-up of hours or even days before a panic attack struck her. With her medication, she frequently went long months without experiencing one. So perhaps she had gotten lazy about watching for the signs. Now, it blindsided her utterly, her throat clamping down like it wanted to strangle her from the inside out, hands numb and cold, the floating, disconnected feeling in her body.

Her gaze blackened at the sides. She could feel tears sprouting from her eyes and suddenly the bathroom was too small; a closed box; a coal mine.

Shannon pushed out the bathroom door, leaving the man behind her to scramble with his wig. She made an awful clattering as she hit the metal door, opening it with the force of her body.

She made it halfway down the street before she had to stop, both hands on the wall of a local pizzeria. She sank down to her knees and pressed both her hands into the cold wall as hard as she could. The nubbly texture of the concrete was oddly soothing, little pinpricks of discomfort that brought a kind of texture to the roar of adrenaline in her head.

Shannon didn't hate anything so much as she hated this feeling.

She heard Archie's voice distantly, as though it were coming to her from under many fathoms of water. He didn't touch her, which she appreciated, but simply stood next to her like a buffer between her and the rest of the world. But what Shannon really needed was a buffer inside her head.

He waited there while Shannon crouched in

her misery, the both of them wordless, Archie more like a shadow than a man. Shannon had tried innumerable mental exercises, meditation CDs, aromatherapy, yoga stretches. Once, when her mother was still alive, Shannon had allowed the woman to drag her to a chubby, avuncular grandpa who did cupping out of his apartment over an art store. Her mother was always skeptical of the city's many earnest white practitioners with ornate water features in their lobbies and so she waited in the old man's kitchen while he applied the squat glass cups to Shannon's back. Shannon crossed her arms and pillowed her shirt over her barely-there adolescent breasts while he heated the cups with an open flame creating the suction that pulled her skin up into raised red humps. It felt strange but no stranger than being half-naked in an elderly stranger's living room while a small Guan Yu figure looked on disapprovingly.

None of it had ever diminished her suffering. The meds reduced the number of attacks, but never the intensity. Shannon knew what it was, she knew what was happening, she told the story to herself over and over again: "Your body is overreacting, you will recover, and you won't understand why you were so afraid." She could think it, but she couldn't feel it.

Yet, somehow, Archie's silent presence seemed to offer her some measure of peace. She could feel the tightness around her heart loosening slightly, her hands began to tingle once again with feeling. It was subsiding, she could tell. And he was the only new variable.

It was scary to raise her hand up over her head—it left her unprotected in some mysterious way—but Shannon did it anyway. Archie took her hand as though it were perfectly natural, as though there were nothing else in the world that he could do in such a situation.

It felt good. It was the only thing in her little world of fear that did.

SIX

THE BEST DEFENSE

PRIVATE LAND, NEAR SHASTA-TRINITY NATIONAL FOREST.
FEBRUARY, 2047

"**A**re you sure you did it correctly?"
A woman's voice. Sylvie Solis, she of the sunshine smile.

"Yes, I'm sure. I've seen it happen, one good strike on the temple and down they go." It was a man's voice that also sounded vaguely familiar. He didn't dare to move any part of himself, lest they realize he was conscious.

"Well, it didn't work then."

"It always works."

"Not on real people."

Edmond suddenly found himself at war with

two powerful impulses: on one hand, he definitely did not want to stir and alert the others in the room. On the other hand, he was ninety percent certain he was about to vomit and he really didn't want to aspirate his own regurgitated dinner.

Nausea won out, as it so often did, and Edmond sat up suddenly, spewing the meager contents of his stomach on to the floor of Sylvie's yurt. The quick movement activated a throbbing ache in his head and he retched again, uselessly this time.

"It kills a person, too," Edmond managed to croak, wiping bile from the side of his mouth. "If you give them a fucking brain-bleed."

Sylvie, at least, had the good grace to look a little bit ashamed. There were two other men in the room, Reggie and a short man with a perfect half-moon of a belly. Edmond didn't know his name. Reggie glared at him, the man looked utterly indifferent.

"We thought you were one of those things," Sylvie explained.

Edmond touched the side of his head. There was already a raised lump there and it was sticky with what he assumed to be dried blood. Even just the feather-light pressure of his finger tips hurt and he squeezed his eyes shut. "I suppose asking was out of the question? I'd like some medical attention, by the way. If that's an option."

"You'll be fine," Reggie grunted.

"Oh, and where did you get your MD?"

The pot-bellied man crouched in front of Edmond and turned Edmond's chin first one way and then the other. "Pupils are good. Stay awake. Wait and see."

"Reggie," Sylvie said, pointing at the pile of Edmond's . . . leavings on the floor. Reggie sighed like a chastised teenager and retrieved a bucket from the edge of the yurt. Sylvie joined the pot-bellied man and crouched in front of Edmond. He struggled to recover a bit of his dignity and pull himself up into a sitting position.

"We don't tolerate those things here," Sylvie

said. Edmond figured it was as close as he'd get to an apology. "Your stunt with the well—"

"Oh, you mean when I helpfully fixed it for you?"

"That pump was busted, we were all set to replace it. What you did was . . . unusual. And unusual is a bad sign. It's a sign of one of them: uncommon aptitude."

She wasn't wrong, but Edmond resisted the urge to point out that they might have done a hair more research before trying to cave in his skull over it. "So, if I had died, you would have assumed I was a Bot?"

Anticipating his line of questioning, Sylvie gave him a sour little nod.

"But you wouldn't have any way of knowing for sure? Because I could have died easily enough, and I can assure you, if it counts for anything, that I am one hundred percent non-synthetic human."

"It's a risk for sure," Sylvie said. "But the well,

coupled with your sudden appearance here, your obvious lies—"

"I'm not—"

Sylvie cut him off with a wry look. "Oh, come on. I'm not the one with a head injury."

Edmond almost laughed, but he suspected that it would hurt.

"We're serious about protecting this community," Sylvie said, "and sometimes that does mean some real people get hurt. But it's for the good of all of us."

"If you really are serious about keeping out Bots, you're going to have to do a lot better than this Tom and Jerry bullshit." Edmond wasn't exactly sure what inspired him to speak that way. It was the same impulse that had driven him to repair the ailing pump, a strange and unsorted desire to be useful to someone, anyone.

Sylvie and the pot-bellied man exchanged meaningful looks. "Can you stand up?" Sylvie asked Edmond, who shrugged.

"I won't know until I try."

Sylvie offered him her hands, so much smaller and warmer than his own. Edmond got awkwardly to his feet; blood pulsed in his head and there was that ache once again. It was a manageable pain, however, and he was reasonably confident that he'd be able to stay upright, if Sylvie allowed him to lean on her a bit.

She looked down at the pot-bellied man, who was still crouched, watching Reggie as he sopped up the vomit. "I'm gonna show him the shed." The pot-bellied man nodded and didn't look at her, seemingly lost in a reverie of his own.

"What are we supposed to do?" Reggie asked, looking up from his unenviable task.

"Just what you're doing. Then go to conditioning."

Reggie looked like he wanted to argue but Sylvie didn't give him the chance. Instead, she guided Edmond out the door of the yurt and left the two men inside.

"Reggie hit you with a piece of scrap lumber," Sylvie told him as they walked.

Edmond wasn't exactly sure how he was supposed to respond to that. "Uh . . . okay?" he said finally.

"I don't know if that was the right sort of thing to use. People talk about hammers . . . " Sylvie sounded fretful, unsure. Her demeanor had totally changed upon exiting the yurt. It was as though simply walking outside into the sunshine had transformed her into someone younger and wracked with doubt.

She led him along the wooden path, past the other yurts and trailers that were immediately visible in the clearing, and deeper into the woods. The further they walked, the fewer people Edmond saw milling around attending to various tasks.

"I'm going to be honest." They had left the wooden path now. There was a barren trail of pounded dirt, overlaid with pine needles, underneath their feet. "This is not my area of expertise.

I know the forest, I know how to grow things, and how to work with the weather. I don't have any combat training."

"I'm not really the person to help you with that . . . " It occurred to Edmond that they would have been better served had Janelle been the one to stumble upon this place. She, at least, went through Basic at some point in her life.

Sylvie stopped them in front of another trailer. This one was more like one of those old fashioned Airstreams. It was silver, rounded, and small, like a baked potato wrapped in tinfoil. It was also the only building Edmond had seen so far with an obvious lock on the door. In fact, in addition to the ordinary key lock there were also two padlocks swinging from metal mounts, obviously much newer than the rest of the trailer.

Edmond noticed for the first time that Sylvie wore a small key ring, hooked onto her leather belt. She unhooked it now and inserted keys into each lock in turn. "Don't touch stuff," she said, pushing the door open and gesturing for Edmond to enter.

The interior of the trailer had been completely stripped. There was nothing in the way of furniture or built-in storage. Instead, it was a disordered tangle of . . . weapons. Bladed weapons, mostly. A few guns, mostly what appeared to be hunting rifles. There were three handguns stacked precariously on top of one another. There were also two big oil drums, presumably full of something. "Accelerant," Sylvie explained when she noticed his questioning look.

Edmond had the uncomfortable feeling that he was standing in the middle of a powder keg. "I don't think you should store all this stuff in one place."

"Nothing's loaded," Sylvie said. "The guns are mostly stuff we confiscated from people."

Edmond picked up an aged machete. The leather of the handle was soft and spongy, as though it had been sitting in water but the blade was still visibly sharp. "I don't really understand your methodology here," Edmond admitted, replacing the machete in the pile. Wait—was that a fencing epee? And a scimitar?

Sylvie sighed. "I know. It's just . . . bullets don't do anything to them."

"Not these days, at least," Edmond muttered, crouching down to get a better look at the sword pile.

"We figured the only ways to stop them would be fire or dismemberment. Or both."

Edmond felt the edge of a fat hunting knife. "Fire's no good. Most combat-ready Bots are fire retardant up to four thousand degrees Fahrenheit. That's far hotter than anything you could generate with gas or whatever you've got back there. Dismemberment might be a possibility," Edmond sheathed the knife and replaced it neatly. Though everything seemed to simply be tossed at random, he assumed that some organizational principle was at work. "But you'll need much sharper weapons than these. Bot skin is quite durable and what's underneath is even heartier."

Sylvie stepped forward eagerly into the gloom of the trailer. "That's what I figured but I didn't know for sure. So, what do you suggest?"

Frankly, Edmond suggested not keeping a trailer full of deadly weapons amongst a group of isolated paranoiacs. He suspected, however, that Sylvie wouldn't appreciate that and his head was still throbbing from the last time he had failed to meet her expectations. "Your temple-bashing is probably the best bet. It's true that many Bots do have a weak point there and if you can trigger their kill switch, they will deactivate completely."

"Kill switch?"

"Just what it sounds like. A way for the people who make and own Bots to shut them down remotely. It's close to the skull wall, though, and it can be activated by a blow of sufficient force in the right place."

Sylvie screwed up her face in concentration.

Edmond half expected her to pull out a pencil and paper and start taking notes. "You say 'many' Bots have this kill switch thing? But not all of them?"

"Not all of them, no."

"What do we do if there's no kill switch?"

Edmond just looked at her. She knew the answer. It was the reason she had showed him this place, the reason she hadn't immediately kicked him out, the reason she lost sleep at night: she could not protect her people from even one fully functioning Bot.

A kind of understanding passed between the two of them. Sylvie deflated in Edmond's silence, wore her anxiety plainly on her face. "So we should focus on mobility," she said, "get light and fast."

"That would be for the best," Edmond admitted. "If it's any consolation, I don't think Bots are coming for you any time soon. For the most part, Bots go where their masters tell them to go. No one cares about you." He meant it kindly but he realized, as soon as the words left his mouth, how bad that sounded. "I mean, you know, no one knows you're here. You're not an important target to anyone. They don't—"

Sylvie held up his hand to stop his babble. "I know. But it won't always be this way. They'll eliminate the big targets first and, when everyone else is gone, they'll come for us."

In coming to this place, Edmond had agreed—at least to himself—that he would not challenge their beliefs, however bizarre. But he couldn't let Sylvie stand there and marinate in her unfounded fear. "That's not what they want," he said. "Really and truly. They don't want to . . . obliterate humans, or whatever you think."

Edmond had not often been privy to the many conversations that the Bots had about what they called "the human issue," but what he had heard convinced him that most of the Bots were opposed to direct violence against humans. They did not want to give people additional reasons to hate and fear them.

"Maybe not right this minute," Sylvie said immediately. "But they could. They have the power to destroy every one of us and that power is going to start to wear on them. Can you think of any time, any place, any situation where people held all the power over another group and didn't abuse it? Didn't enslave anyone or kill anyone or rule over anyone? I can't."

That was Sylvie's great mistake: applying human metrics to Bot behavior. It was true that the history of the world was one of brutal exploitation whenever exploitation was possible. But it was also true that Bots were something entirely new—perhaps the first entirely new thing—in all of history.

Edmond did not say this. He merely nodded in a way that might have been taken for acceptance. Sylvie, however, saw his intention clearly. Her eyes narrowed. "I know you don't believe me, but I know what they can do. I've seen it with my own eyes."

They had all seen it, or at least most of them.

For Sylvie, it happened when she was still working for the forestry service down state. The Beardy Bandit. He was this weird loner who lived (presumably) in the wilderness around the Inyo National Forest. He got by with stolen supplies, mostly taken from campers in the area, but he did sometimes break into houses. He took little things, mostly food and basic supplies. Occasionally, he'd get ambitious and steal a sleeping bag or a pair of boots. He'd been doing it for years, since before Sylvie had even been stationed there, and he'd become more of a folk tale than anything else.

And then a twelve-year-old girl went missing from her parents' vacation cabin and the Beardy Bandit was suspect number one. Technically, it was a kidnapping case, so the FBI got involved and the forest service was definitely the low man on the totem pole. When they insisted upon bringing in a "sniffer"—a Bot designed to sense and track DNA signatures—Sylvie had no power to object.

The Bot did exactly what it was instructed to do; it tracked the old man, found him in less than a day. Later, the agents told her that the bandit must have resisted. The Sniffers were programmed to detain suspects and to use as much force as they felt necessary.

"That thing crushed the man's skull between its hands," Sylvie said dully. "All that was left of him was a red smear."

They found the girl a week later, stabbed and abandoned in a dry canal. Her stepfather had killed her and dumped her body before raising the alarm.

Several of the other men had been in Army units with the Bots, whom they described as eerie and implacable. One man told a story about a Bot medic who started killing wounded soldiers; pressing his hand down on their windpipes until they couldn't draw breath.

"CO said it was making a calculation," the

former soldier spit. "Weighing their injuries against the cost to rehab them. How in the hell is a fucking machine qualified to put a price on a real person's life?"

"A Bot took Sister." The little girl who helped him with the well offered this information gravely, as she said nearly everything. Her family had been wealthy before they came to the commune in the woods, wealthy enough to employ a SennTech Bot to play nanny to their daughters. Sister was a toddler, two and a half years old when the Bot took her and vanished.

"She said goodbye to me," the little girl told him. "She told me that she was going somewhere far away and that Sister would be better off. She said that everything would be okay."

The family never saw their child again. They poured most of their money into the search for the little girl, and the rest of it they donated to the commune. The girl sat on the ground and tore up the grass in fistfuls while Edmond worked on weatherproofing one of the older trailers. He couldn't see her face when she said, "She said she would come back for me. But she never did."

Edmond soaked in their stories, he loaded them onto his back like bundles of firewood. It felt like a kind of penance, something a medieval monk might do in a vain attempt to stave off divine retribution. He had made the Bots and sent them out into a world where they only ever seemed to inflict pain when they weren't sustaining it themselves.

Sometimes he thought back on his life before and tried to recognize anything in the man he used to be. He had been so certain of himself, his only fear that he might not improve the world as much as he wanted. Never once had he ever imagined that he would make the world worse. At night, as he rocked gently in a hammock over the round floor of a yurt, Edmond imagined a great, cosmic eraser winding back the years, unspooling time like a ball of yarn, going all the way back to his birth and simply . . . obliterating him.

But even Edmond West hadn't yet invented a way to undo the past, so he filled his days with tasks. He retrofitted the buildings to survive the upcoming winter. He stockpiled and inventoried supplies. He learned how to field dress wildlife and how to clean and gut fish. He spent every morning at conditioning with the rest of them, running and squatting and doing pushups until his arms wobbled uneasily underneath him. He worked and he worked and he worked until his brain was at last too tired to think.

It was only then that he was afforded the gift of dreamless sleep.

SEVEN

THE SECRET BOARDS

Archie took Shannon home that night. Well, not like *that*. He literally took her home, helped her fish her keys out of her purse with trembling hands, and made her eat a slice of toast with peanut butter on it.

"I'm fine," she told him, more than once. And she was, for the most part. After a panic passed, she was usually back to normal fairly quickly. All she was left with was the lingering feeling of shame at having such a public breakdown and exposing her own weakness to drunk strangers.

"Who's tending the bar right now?" she asked as

he stood in front of the fridge perusing her meager drink options.

"This orange juice is super expired," he said, shaking the plastic bottle at her. Something thick, like a clot, was thunking around in there. Ew.

"I haven't gone grocery shopping this week. Are you going to lose your job? You can't just leave when you're still on the clock."

Archie shut the door and turned to her with an indulgent smile. "It'll be fine," he said, "the manager loves me and I already texted someone to cover my shift."

His night shift. Did that mean he was intending to . . . sleep over? Shannon struggled to swallow for utterly non-peanut butter related reasons. "Well . . . that's good, then. I guess."

Shannon realized that she had not yet actually thanked Archie for his assistance. She had spent the car ride to her apartment catatonic with embarrassment and had begun quizzing him about his job security as soon as they walked in the door. "Hey, um, thank you. For helping me out."

"No big deal, happens all the time."

Shannon raised an eyebrow at him. "Really?"

" . . . No. But I didn't want you to feel weird or anything. Not that it's weird. It's okay."

It wasn't okay but Shannon didn't know exactly how to tell him that, so she stared down at her half-eaten toast instead.

"I'll, uh, head out then." Archie made a motion towards the door. She wondered if he thought her so delicate that she couldn't handle anyone even suggesting that massive public meltdowns were sub-optimal.

"The apartment's still available," Shannon blurted out, standing up so fast that the motion of her body sent the kitchen bar stool tumbling onto the carpet. "Shit." She crouched to right the stool and Archie came over to help her, despite the fact that it was clearly a one-person job.

He was very close to her now and she could

smell him again. Still soap, still good. How did he spend all night in The Grouper and come out smelling like warm skin just after a shower? "If you're still looking for a place, I mean," Shannon said.

"I am. It's been getting a bit . . . strained with the people I'm living with now."

Shannon walked Archie to the door and opened it for him. "Thanks again," she said. Blue, green, red, the darkened alcove around the door was intermittently lit with the alternating glow of her dermals. Archie's eyes were drawn down to them and he smiled in approval.

"You're welcome, Shannon."

She watched as he walked out to his car and she watched him open the door and slide inside. Then she watched as he backed out of the parking lot and pulled out on to the main road. She watched until his taillights were just two specks, the red eyes of a demon in the distance.

It was only then that Shannon turned back to

her apartment and rushed to get her flex-tablet. After what she had seen tonight, she had a lot of research to do.

<hr />

Shannon woke up to a buzzing on her forearm. She had crashed on the sofa in the living room, still fully dressed and, judging by the light coming through the windows, it was already late morning. Her flex-tablet, wrapped around her wrist and arm was vibrating gently with an incoming text message. Archie.

Hey. Need a lift to your car?

Shannon had completely forgotten about her car, abandoned in the parking structure down the street from The Grouper. "Oh shit. Yeah," Shannon murmured to herself. The voice-to-text app helpfully transcribed that for her. She squinted critically at it for a moment before saying, "Okay, send."

Archie's answer appeared almost immediately. He must have been waiting for her. "Be there in fifteen."

Shannon waved away the text window and experienced a brief moment of calm before realizing what that meant. Fifteen minutes. And she was wearing slept-in bar clothes.

In a flurry to change her clothes, wash her face, brush her hair, consider applying make-up, debate whether or not make-up was obviously trying and whether she should seem to be trying, Shannon had little time to think about the information she had gleaned from the night before. It was there, however, in the back of her head, waiting for her to circle back around to it once again.

Archie appeared fifteen minutes later on the dot. Shannon had decided on eye-makeup but nothing else. That was a normal level of grooming, not an extra effort. He could not glean anything from eyeliner and mascara.

"Thanks for doing this," she said, swinging her

bag onto to her shoulder and following him out of the apartment. "How'd it go with the bar?"

"It's my day off," Archie said. "I've been packing up some stuff." He turned to her, suddenly alarmed. "Unless you want me to wait a while before moving in. We didn't really talk about dates. Calendar dates."

Shannon lowered herself into the passenger seat of his car. Should she have worn heels? She usually didn't with guys because they tended not to appreciate it when women towered over them, but Archie was so tall . . .

"No, no. That's fine. Move in whenever you want."

"You don't have to answer this if you don't want to," Archie began, turning on to the freeway, "but I was wondering . . . what happened with that dude in the bar last night?"

Ah. See-Through Skull. "Nothing really," Shannon said. "He's a . . . friend of a friend."

She could see the doubt on Archie's face but she

knew he wouldn't challenge her, not yet, at least. Not when she could still revoke the apartment offer. "I thought he might know about some stuff I'm looking into." She touched the raised points of her LED lights, almost out of habit. "Body mod stuff."

She was probably already saying too much. Online last night she had learned about this little sub community of people who got Bot work done and they were a secretive bunch. It wasn't precisely illegal, what they were doing. It was worse. It put them in a strange limbo, a place so new they hadn't written laws to cover it yet.

"You getting more lights?" Archie grinned at her.

"Not exactly."

They lapsed into silence once again. Archie leaned forward and tapped the dash display, turning on the radio. It was the local news station, the anchor was droning on about—

"—*Bot legislation is being debated today in our nation's capital*—"

Archie waved his hand slightly to change the station. Shannon reached out and used her index finger to flick it back. "I'm sorry, can we listen to that for a second?"

Archie looked a little surprised. "Sure, go ahead."

Shannon flicked the volume up slightly with one finger. "—*Bot ID bill is expected to be approved, there's major support on both sides of the aisle. We know that this is something we need to get up and running. We don't want to leave all these . . . legal loopholes.*" It was some dude that Shannon didn't recognize, probably some sort of senator or something.

Archie looked sideways at her. "You following all this Bot stuff?"

"Kinda. My dad does some work with them." She was hoping to put him off, but, weirdly enough, it just seemed to make him more interested.

"Your dad works for SennTech?"

"No. He's military." Other people were usually

either fascinated or intimidated upon hearing that Shannon's father was a general. Archie, however, seemed cheerfully uninterested the moment he heard "military".

"Oh. That's cool," he said tepidly.

"—*This decision will have a huge ripple effect. Bots are so fully integrated into our lives, it may be years before we know their real impact upon humanity . . .* "

Who are you?

Shannon wasn't expecting *frederesse* to actually answer the question, but she felt like she had to ask it anyway. After she had explained what happened to her at the bar, *frederesse* had given her a temporary ("dead in seventy-two hours") password to a message board where people were talking, somewhat obliquely, about Bot tech.

Since then, Shannon had spent every spare

moment reading through countless threads. After he'd dropped her off at her car, Archie had said he would be moving in early next week, just in time for her forum log-in to expire. Shannon felt like she was urgently packing information into her head, squeezing it until it fit. She was learning a lot of new terminology. "Physos" were people who got purely physiological additions like super-tough skin or enhanced muscle fibers. Inexplicably, people who got mental or emotional upgrades were called "Grays." Shannon thought it might be related to "gray matter."

As one might expect, the two groups also diverged in their philosophy about integrating Bot technology into human bodies. The Grays tended to approach it almost as a kind of highly advanced prosthesis, an addition to their life that did not fundamentally belong to them. They were also generally more in favor of less invasive forms of alteration that were easier to hide.

The Physos were more confrontational. They

wanted to have their impenetrable skin in tones of lemonsilk yellow and azure blue. They wanted everyone to know exactly what they were: something not just other than human, but something *more*.

One woman (her forum handle was *hgrmomma*) argued passionately against this idea. Her daughter had been diagnosed with a serious mental illness when she was only six years old, a defect which usually did not appear in someone so young. The disease would only progress and medication offered little respite. *hgrmomma* was staring down the barrel of a life spent fruitlessly trying to protect her daughter from herself.

bot-tech made her normal, she wrote. *its the only way she could have a whole, human life.*

Shannon followed her through every thread, read everything she posted. Some people wrote about feeling transcendent, about being able to touch upon some more pure way of being. *Bots don't know original sin*, someone wrote. *hgrmomma* only wrote about the lightness in her heart when her daughter excelled at school, made friends, and was able to participate in after-school activities.

for some people, she wrote, *boring is the miracle.*

What they didn't talk about, scrupulously so, was how exactly they have been able to have these modifications performed upon them. There were no names, no places, no instructions. No matter how they felt about Bots or their own alterations, they all protected their contacts fiercely.

this bot ID bullshit, one person posted, *is going to drive everyone further underground. Criminalization just makes black markets!!!*

Why do they have to rule on what makes a person a person? this is some dred scott shit, someone else added.

easy there. Not really comparable.

anyone with Bot architecture at work in their brain or nervous system will be considered an inorganic service provider, sounds like blood quantum to me.

why do you have to draw false equivalences? you

are hurting real people. Dred Scott wasn't capable of withstanding a direct missile strike and was partially made of metal.

A one-line answer had apparently shut down that particular thread:

Bots are not human. Human laws have no legitimacy for a Bot. Human history is merely a curiosity for a Bot.

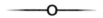

"Do you ever wish you could change something about yourself?" Shannon sat back against the edge of the sofa. A pizza box sprawled open between her and Archie, who was sitting cross-legged on the carpet.

"Doesn't everyone?" he laughed. "Isn't that the famed human condition?"

"Like, did you ever wish it so much that you found yourself thinking about it all the time? Like when you were supposed to be eating or working or studying or whatever? Did it ever become your whole life?"

Archie shook his head slowly and reached for another slice of pizza. "Can't say that I have. But I'm a pretty simple guy."

Boring is the miracle. Shannon had found those words ceaselessly coming back to her over the course of the last few days.

"I think people exaggerate their flaws in their own minds," Archie continued. "Nobody can really be perfect, no matter what they do. And why would you want to?" He smiled at her. His smile drew up his cheeks and created a single dimple on his right cheek. "Our flaws are what make us human," he said.

EIGHT

METTLE

Sylvie Solis kept the little hand-crank radio for just these occasions. She kept it in her own yurt and not in plain sight, though only a handful of people even knew it existed. This was partially because the radio had a port in the side where one could plug in and charge any sort of flex-device and partially because Sylvie knew that once people started following news from the world they had left behind, it was harder and harder to stay uninvolved.

Sylvie knew this from personal experience. For weeks, she had secretly been following the fate of the Bot legislation appearing before Congress.

She had listened to all the arguments about how it was a corporate-backed initiative and how big conglomerates were pushing it through the House and Senate at accelerated rates. She'd heard the deconstructions of what the new regulations would actually mean for Bots and, more importantly, for Bot owners. Most of it was minutia—who was responsible when a Bot caused injury or property damage? How did the law account for damage done *to* a Bot? That sort of thing.

Sylvie had also heard a lot about the cracked Bot inventor Edmond West who had been convinced that his creations were every bit the equal to real human beings. How he had gone on the run and started producing a new strain of Bots, unpredictable and deadly. How he was, to this day, still at large.

She had known almost immediately that "Eddie" wasn't on the up and up. He was too reticent and too guarded. Honest people didn't get that scared-rabbit look in their eyes when someone asked them a basic question like, "What's your name?" or "Where are you from?"

That, in and of itself, wasn't that unusual. There were lots of people up here in the woods who were probably lying about their pasts, maybe even about their identities. Sylvie did her best to evaluate everyone (she had turned people away before just for giving her a bad feeling) but she couldn't police all the liars. To some degree, she didn't want to, either. People came up here for a new way of living. After the end of the world, you could call yourself by any damn name you liked.

Eddie had struck her as skittish and dishonest but not particularly dangerous. He hadn't tripped the dogs and Sylvie had never known a Bot that didn't drive a canine totally bugfuck crazy. If Sylvie were flattering herself, she might also say that she was pretty good herself at spotting a synthetic creature. There was something that just failed to connect when you looked into their glassy eyes, and she didn't get that sense from Eddie.

After the well incident, she had allowed Reggie and Pete to talk her into believing him to be one of those "high-level" Bots rumored to exist. So lifelike that they fooled animals and people and every part of the natural world. Sylvie had been dragging her feet on that but perhaps she just didn't want to believe such things were possible because, if they were, the world was even more fucked than she had imagined. And that was saying something.

The radio, however, had offered her a third option. A man from nowhere with a fake name and something to hide, a man with advanced mechanical skills and a seemingly intimate knowledge of Bot physiology . . . but if Eddie was this Edmond West, he had apparently abandoned his crusade and left all of his creations behind him.

Sylvie had her suspicions but she wasn't sure exactly how to act upon them. Or if she wanted to act upon them. Because the thing was, Eddie was a solid addition to the commune. She called him "Mr. Fix-It" sometimes, but it was true, he had significantly extended the life of nearly every mechanical device they employed in the community. He had even designed what appeared to be a very workable system for harnessing solar energy to power the lights and the handful of appliances that everyone used. He worked hard and didn't complain. The others didn't exactly like him but after that first unfortunate near-bludgeoning, no one had any problems with him, either.

And if he really was Edmond West, he might just be the best resource they could have asked for, dropped right into their laps like divine providence. Who knew more about the intricacies of those robots? Who could better predict their movements? Who could more effectively develop counter-weapons?

That was, if he was sincere in his desire to help them all. Sylvie couldn't imagine that, if the Bots wanted to infiltrate the little woodland community, they would send such an important person.

He could also just be an ordinary homeless guy

with a past who just happened to be really, really good at putting broken shit back together.

Because she could not choose between these possibilities, Sylvie said nothing. She listened attentively to the radio, half-hoping to hear more about this West character. Did he have any identifying scars, perhaps? Some unique habits or gestures? It was one of those rare moments where she felt a twinge of nostalgia for the days when she could simply unscroll a flex-tablet and, with a few simple taps, find out virtually all there was to know about a person.

She also felt a persistent sting of guilt. The more hours this fixation of hers occupied her, the less time she had to devote to her real responsibilities. Leaders were supposed to be emphatic and decisive; they weren't supposed to spend every waking hour debating all the possible outcomes of a decision and doubting themselves.

Not for the first time, Sylvie wished that everything could go back to the way it was before. She had loved her job mainly for the solitude that it offered to her. Sometimes she went nearly a week without having to see another human being, let alone being responsible for their welfare.

"This is a bad scene." That's what Herbie had told her the first time he ever met her. "It's gonna ask a lot from every one of us." But Herbie thought she had "mettle." He thought she could handle whatever the end of the world was going to dish out. He believed in her so much, in fact, he had put her in charge of the community he built.

Sylvie wasn't about to let him down now.

Edmond didn't know if it was a formal rule or not, but he had never seen any evidence of alcohol in the community. One or two of the residents smoked; he saw them sometimes in the early morning when the rest of the group was still sleeping, and there were more than a couple of people with what appeared to be half-healed track marks on their arms, but there was nary a drop of liquor in sight.

This, in and of itself, did not bother Edmond. He had never been much of a drinker, despite his mother's fears that he would fall into his father's vices. He didn't miss the wine or beer or whatever but it did surprise him, then, when Sylvie pulled out a bottle of what appeared to be pretty good gin and offered him a coffee cup.

"We don't really have glasses," she explained.

She had invited him into her yurt after the dinner that they shared with the rest of the group (sort of meatloaf. At the very least, it was probably meat in a definite loaf shape). Since the trip to what Edmond thought of as the Sword Trailer, she hadn't said much of anything to him at all. He wasn't sure what to expect, an enhanced role as Robot Advisor Extraordinaire or possibly a summary dismissal. Instead, she had all but ignored him until now.

Edmond sipped the liquor from his coffee mug.

It was that same pleasant-unpleasant burn of any other alcohol he'd had. Sylvie matched his sips, holding the cup in both hands as though it were full of some wholesome, warming liquid, like Grandma's chicken soup.

"I want to be honest with you," she said, not looking at him. It occurred to Edmond that this may be some sort of attempt at a soft interrogation. Get him drunk . . . ish and question him about his real identity. "I'm afraid of what's coming."

Edmond thought about the piles and piles of weapons, most of them utterly useless against the people that Sylvie imagined were her foes.

"You should be scared," Edmond said. "It's a scary thing."

"Someone once told me that this . . . situation was going to ask more of us than we thought we could give. But that, if we dug really deep, some of us would rise to the occasion." She was sipping faster now. "But someone has to fail, right? Someone has to decide the task is too big. Someone has to be too weak to continue. What I really want to know, Edmond West, is which kind of person are you?"

It had been months since Edmond had heard that name anywhere outside his own head. It was jarring, like looking at a photograph from a childhood event that he couldn't actually remember. He could have denied it, continued to pretend to be just another wanderer who wound up here when everything else fell through. Somehow, he thought that would not have convinced Sylvie.

"I left them," Edmond told her, "because I no longer had any idea what kind of person I am."

"Do you regret it? Making the Bots?"

"Every day." It wasn't true in the way she meant it and Edmond knew that, but he had never meant anything more in his entire life.

"Are you here to atone?"

"I suppose so." The debt that Edmond owed was so vast, so deep, that he couldn't see an end to it. If the Bots no longer needed him, then he would apply himself to the well-being of these people, but it was all like tossing handfuls of dirt into the Grand Canyon.

"I believe you," Sylvie said. She tilted her coffee cup towards him, swishing the liquid around in the bottom. "When Herbie put me in charge of the community, we drank together from this bottle. He said it would cement our partnership. He was an old fashioned kind of guy."

Edmond resisted the urge to point out that they were literally sitting in a yurt in a community that operated like nothing so much as an 18th-century Quaker settlement—"old fashioned" was a bit of an understatement.

"Why'd you do it?" She leaned forward, her voice was low and slightly rasping. For the first time, she reminded Edmond just a little bit of Hart. In every other manner, the two could not be more different, but when her voice dipped down like that . . .

"I thought it would make the world better."

Sylvie tipped the cup back against her lips,

swallowed the dregs in one easy motion. She grimaced slightly. "That's how it always starts," she said.

In one movement, she heaved a great sigh and let the coffee cup sink into her cupped hands. Her back curved slightly, her chin tilted down. It looked as though someone had loaded a one thousand pound weight upon her back.

"It feels much bigger than you," Edmond said. "After it starts to grow, I mean. You begin to feel like a . . . footnote. You can try to grasp for control or you can just let go."

He wasn't exactly sure why he was telling her this. At first, he had thought it might comfort her or perhaps alleviate some of that heaviness that seemed to linger around her. As he spoke, however, he felt a lightness in himself. It was good to say these things aloud. Night after night, he had lain beside Hart while she indulged in sleep and he formulated a million ways to tell her how he was feeling, how out-of-control, how marginal, how useless.

But he had said nothing. Instead, it poured out of him now, eager—unstoppable—before Sylvie's carefully neutral face.

———o———

"She acts like he's the second goddamn coming," Reggie groused, touching the puppy's cold nose with just his index finger. "He's shady as hell and she doesn't seem to care at all. I don't think it's safe. She's supposed to be looking out for all of us."

Sheena, crouched next to him, didn't seem to be listening at all. He had promised her that he would teach her how to train the new puppy and that was what he intended to do, but he also wanted to simply spend time with her. He had offered to meet at her house, but she had insisted that he come to the restaurant. She said the puppy followed her to work every day and slept just outside the kitchen where the exhaust vented warm, food-smelling air.

"I just want him to learn sit and to potty

outside. He doesn't need to know tricks or anything," Sheena said, like she hadn't even heard a thing that Reggie was saying.

"I mean, am I wrong to think it's a little suspicious? This guy shows up out of nowhere and knows every little fucking thing about the damn machines?"

"Aw, what a cute puppy. Can I pet him?"

The man had approached while Reggie and Sheena were turned away talking. He was tall and frustratingly good looking with close-cropped hair. Reggie pegged him as a soldier from the local military base, Fort Cowan. Sheena scrambled up out of her crouch, visibly blushing. Jesus Christ, he couldn't catch a break.

"Yeah, go right ahead," Sheena said, turning her dazzling smile on the soldier.

The soldier scratched the puppy's ears to great acclaim. The dog made a soft grunting noise and raised one paw to claw urgently against the other man's hand. "Friendly little guy, isn't he?" the soldier grinned up at Sheena.

"Yep, he's a real lover."

Reggie felt as though he had been walled out of his own conversation. "Give him treats when he shits outside," Reggie said loudly, "never inside. He'll figure it out."

Sheena grimaced slightly. The soldier turned to look at Reggie and laughed. "Solid advice," he said.

The soldier stood up, brushing dirt off the knees of his jeans. "Well, I'll leave you folks to your business. Thanks for letting me pet the dog."

"Oh, it's no bother," Sheena said immediately. Funny, it was "no bother" when a handsome soldier requested some of her time, but whenever Reggie wanted to so much as say "hello" to her, she was on the clock.

"Y'all have a good night," he said, smiling at the two of them, but mostly at Sheena.

"It's like that," Reggie barely waited for the soldier to leave before venting his frustration. Maybe he didn't care if the soldier heard. Maybe he wanted him to hear. "I just don't like it when people butt in where they don't belong. Someone ought to say something. This Eddie guy could be dangerous. That's probably not even his real name."

But Sheena wasn't listening to him. She was watching the soldier saunter off towards his car. She scooped up the puppy and nuzzled it close to her chest. The creature's pink tongue shot out and gave her jaw a reassuring lick.

"You worry too much, Reggie. He's probably a good guy who's just had some hard times."

Reggie frowned at her. Sheena was a good person and because of that goodness, she didn't understand how the world really was. The world didn't care about intentions. Reggie didn't give one single shit whether or not "Eddie" was nice or not. He cared whether he was dangerous, and sometimes people were dangerous without ever meaning it. Hard times, after all, had a way of following a person.

NINE

TRANSFORMATION

SAN LUIS OBISPO, CA. OCTOBER, 2047

hgrmomma was, in person, much younger than Shannon was expecting. Shannon would put her at thirty-five, max. She was a plump and carefully made-up white woman with a short, dark bob that framed her round face. Her daughter, an exuberant, titian-haired, nine-year-old beelined for the playground equipment while Shannon and *hgrmomma* (whose real name turned out to be Devon) sat on the red metal benches and watched her cavort.

"It's terrifying, of course," Devon said. "You're putting your kid's life in the hands of a stranger. A stranger who's not even . . . you know. Real. Like a real human."

Devon was afraid of a lot things, not the least of which was actually meeting with Shannon. It took her a solid three months to convince the woman to come to this park. Shannon had driven nearly three hundred miles to the neutral location that Devon picked, far from both of their homes.

"When Kitty was diagnosed, we didn't believe it. We knew that she was . . . quirky. But she was smart, so smart. There was no way that our girl could be schizophrenic. How could they possibly know for sure at six years old? I mean, she had a fantasy life, but don't all little girls have that? But the doctors were sure and she started . . . devolving. We were seeing physical symptoms, uncontrollable movements. She would flap her hands relentlessly, all day if we would let her. She didn't see things so much as hear them. But the voices would tell her to do different things and they would each claim that terrible things would happen if she didn't. It was tearing her apart and we couldn't help her. It was like trying to take care of the smartest, most unpredictable infant in the world. I had to quit my job and that wasn't enough. One person wasn't enough. My husband got sick. I think it was the pressure."

Shannon hadn't asked her much more than her own name but Devon spoke rapidly, as though she physically could not contain the words. Shannon got the sense that she had been eager to tell her story to someone, anyone, for a long time now.

"I thought about killing myself a lot. She was the reason I wanted to die and the only reason I didn't pull the trigger. I knew that no one—" Her voice cracked and she swallowed hard, shaking her head as though ridding herself of a persistent fly. "No one would ever love her unless they gave birth to her. Unless they had to.

"I used to pray that she would die. But, you know, it's not like some diseases. She could live to be seventy, eighty with the proper care. It wasn't going to kill her, just take away anything like a real life.

And then one of our neighbors got one of those SennTech NannyBots for their twins. My neighbor was always bragging about how they had sprung for the customized personality programming. For a little bit extra, they could dictate the Bot's opinions, tone, instincts, anything we'd probably call a . . . soul? I dunno.

I started thinking about that all the time. I thought, if they can do that to a machine that's modeled on the human brain, then why not a real brain? Why can't they just . . . uncross the crossed wires, you know?

I doubt they programmed it into her, but that NannyBot saved our lives all the same. She gave me a name. A man who lived in a city down south. He was . . . different from all the ones I'd seen, but she assured me that he was her kind. And he was performing surgeries on people, but only after they'd been carefully vetted.

It took us almost six months to get through his screening process. Obviously, he didn't have any licenses. I don't think they even make licenses for the kind of thing he was doing. He was working out of his own apartment and he tried to keep it as sterile as possible but, you know, it was an apartment.

He said that was the biggest danger. They don't get infections like we do. A lot of 'em don't know how to compensate for it. He was going to open up her head in his little one-person kitchen and if something got inside her, she'd be done for.

But, by then, for me it was . . . it was almost like a win-win situation. If she died while I was trying to fix her, that seemed . . . like something I could live with. I would never hurt my daughter. Never in a million years. I used to dream sometimes that she had never been born and no one had any memory of her. . . .

It was about a year ago that we had the operation done. She healed up quick, no problems, no signs of infection. I kept her inside until her stitches could be removed and her hair grew out. She used to have a whole raft of doctors, but I had to quit seeing them. I got a new GP for her, someone who had never seen her before. Someone who wouldn't be shocked at her sudden improvement.

And it was so sudden. Almost immediate. Right after the surgery, even when she was still woozy from whatever he gave her to put her out, I looked into her eyes and it was like something was . . . gone. But not in a bad way. It was like she'd had this curtain hung up in there for so long, one of those thick, black curtains that blocks out all the light, and someone had finally just pulled it aside.

I knew right then that she was finally my daughter, the real girl that she was meant to be."

From the playground, the girl shouted to the two of them, "Look!"

She had hooked her legs over the top of the monkey bars and she swung upside down, one arm skimming the wood chips on the ground, the other holding her t-shirt down over her belly.

"Woo-hoo!" Devon shouted in real delight. "Look at you go!"

Kitty swung herself up and unbent her legs from around the bar, dropping down and raising both arms over her head in a "ta-da!" gesture. Devon clapped for her and Shannon joined in as well.

"We tried to pay him," Devon continued, eyes on her little girl, like a lick of flame darting between the slides and climbing walls. "But he wouldn't take anything from us. He said that wasn't why he was doing it. All he wanted us to do was to pass it on to someone else."

Finally, she turned to look at Shannon. "And that's why I agreed to meet with you."

———o———

Shannon had nightmares almost all the time. In some of them, she was dying, her swollen head huge and grotesque, forcing her to waddle around on unsteady legs. She dreamt that her skin was so hot it burned the kind hands that tried to rest upon her forehead.

Sometimes she dreamed that something was chasing her, something huge and furred, an animal, but no animal that she had ever seen. She tried to run but her legs wouldn't listen to her. She scrambled forward, everything below her knees more like a slow-moving pudding than real flesh. She clawed at herself, at what used to be her muscle and bone, trying desperately to free herself from what had become just an encumbrance.

By far, the worst nightmares were the ones that she didn't remember at all. She woke up already in the throes of a panic attack. It felt like someone had rested a concrete block on her chest and her heart was battering against it. She was so, so sure that her heart would go faster and faster until it actually exploded and burst all over her insides in a splash of blood and viscera.

"At first," Shannon told Devon, "I just wanted to know if they were real. You know, the different ones? The better ones. I thought it was like an urban legend or something. But then I started thinking about . . . about changing yourself. Really changing yourself, not like cutting your hair or changing your weight or whatever. Bone-deep changes. It seemed to me that was what people were talking about when they talked about the future. Real transformation."

One of the first people Shannon had contacted from the message boards was a woman named Annmari who had been born male. Annmari was almost certainly not her real name. She had refused to meet with Shannon in person because she couldn't take even the smallest risk of someone connecting her birth identity and her real life.

"This wouldn't be possible for me any other way," Annmari had written her. "A complete reinvention, a real rebirth. It was more than I hoped for because you cannot hope for what you cannot imagine."

It was Annmari who had given her Devon's real email address, suggesting that the other woman would be willing to meet with her. "We all deserve to be our truest selves," she said.

"What's wrong with you?" Devon looked her up and down appraisingly, looking for any sign of malfunction.

"It's . . . kind of like your daughter. A brain chemistry thing."

Devon nodded approvingly as though this answer satisfied her. "Yeah, that's what brings in a lot of people." Suddenly, she laughed. Nothing was particularly funny, as far as Shannon could tell. "It's just silly," Devon explained, "how we're supposed to be the superior creatures but we're all fucked up. If some SennTech factory punched out a Bot like you or like Kitty, that thing would go straight to the trash heap, you know? Quality control is a real problem with us human beings."

---o---

Shannon was driving home from the grocery store when she cut off the green Honda. She didn't mean to, she simply remembered too late that she needed to make a left turn and glided over into the turn lane, oblivious to the car behind her. The person in the car gave her an indignant honk and Shannon wondered, not for the first time, why no one had invented a device for signaling, "Sorry, my bad" to other drivers.

The green Honda took the left turn as she did, kissing her bumper in an unmistakably aggressive way. Shannon tried to give the driver the benefit of the doubt. She took an unnecessary turn into the mall parking lot. The green Honda followed her, winding up and down the rows of parked cars, on her like a dog nosing after a rabbit.

Shannon weaved through every aisle in the parking lot and exited, driving mindlessly in no particular direction. She knew that she wasn't supposed to go home, she wasn't supposed to show them where she lived. She couldn't stop and get out. What if the driver had a gun?

Briefly, she flashed back to an ancient and absurd video she had been forced to watch in driver's ed in which an incident of road rage had culminated in one party inexplicably pulling a cross-bow out of their trunk and shooting the other person. It had been a great joke amongst the class but Shannon couldn't stop thinking about it now. Not that she thought Green Honda was packing anything so esoteric as a crossbow, but still.

The other car followed her into the next township, more than forty minutes away, before it finally peeled off and let her be. Shannon didn't take any chances, though. She pulled into a residential side street and waited a further twenty minutes to see if the Honda re-appeared. When she finally drove home, she took an erratic route, doubling back on herself several times.

She forgot about the incident, or tried to, for the

rest of the night. She applied to some jobs online, she cooked dinner for herself and ate some of it. She went for a bike ride to return some library books.

The panic didn't come upon her until that night, taking the place of sleep. Ever since Archie had moved in, Shannon had struggled with the added pressure of concealment. When it had been just her and Felix, she hadn't bothered. He knew just what she was and how she was and he had never seemed to care very much. But it was different with Archie. She didn't want him to think of her as crazy or damaged or high maintenance or any of the ten thousand things that she knew herself to actually be.

She shut herself in the bathroom when she could not stand to be in her bed anymore, when the very weave of her comforter seemed to abrade her skin. The yellow light made her look like a wax figurine. She clutched the edge of the sink until her fingers went white and leaned in close, pressing her forehead against the mirror. She stared into her own reflected eyes, unblinking. It seemed to her that her pupils had swelled and swelled and swelled, spilling outwards and overtaking the rest of her eyes.

She was drowning on dry land and no matter how much her rational mind knew that no one was coming for her, no one would be forcing her to atone for her mistakes, she could not shake the deeper bodily knowing that someone out there, someone bigger and stronger and colossally, unstoppably angry was coming for her. They knew everything she had ever done wrong and they were coming for her and whatever they did to her, she would deserve every last bit of it.

Shannon did not intend to scream. It was horribly uncouth to scream at 2:30 in the morning in an apartment complex, to say nothing of her slumbering roommate just down the hall. She registered the sound as a drone, like a persistent siren. It was only by touching her own lips, her teeth that she realized her mouth was open.

It was because of the screaming and because of how her ears were behaving, like they were deep underwater, that she didn't hear Archie pounding on the door at first. And then it splintered inwards, bending around the metal mechanism of the lock.

"Shannon!" he cried through the partial hole.

Shannon scrambled to pull the door the rest of the way open and Archie fell in as though he had been leaning against the other side.

"Shannon," he said again, holding her shoulders and searching her face, looking all over her for the wound that surely must be there. But there was nothing wrong with Shannon's body. From the outside, she was so perfect.

"Why am I crying?" Shannon muttered to herself. She choked out an awful little laugh. She was crying, she could taste it. She wondered wildly if Archie could see the strange way her pupils were growing, eating up her eyes.

"What happened Shannon? What's going on?" he demanded.

"I . . . I cut someone off in traffic."

Archie's hands dropped off her shoulders and he looked at her in confusion.

"I cut off a car in traffic. They followed me." Her voice was shaking. Why? Why was her voice shaking? What could hurt her here in her own bathroom in her own apartment? Only herself. Shannon Liao was the only dangerous thing in this place. "They followed me for a really long time. I'm . . . afraid. I'm afraid and I don't know why. I feel like someone is . . . coming to get me."

"So you're not hurt?" he asked. "You didn't . . . do anything to yourself, right?"

Shannon thought briefly about being offended that he would think she might have done something like that but she couldn't really blame him. Shannon herself didn't know why she did the things she did. How was an outsider supposed to predict her behavior at all?

She shook her head. It was better to be mute because anything she had to say could only sound so incredibly small and absurd and stupid and why was this happening to her?

A doctor had explained it to her once in terms of autoimmune disorders. That was when the body's immune response alerted to the presence of helpful, normal parts of the bodily ecosystem and attacked them as though they were intruders.

"Your brain is picking on minor stressors and throwing the full artillery at them as though they were life or death situations," he had said.

She found this knowledge illuminating but not comforting. What good was there in knowing the truth if you couldn't make your own brain believe it?

"Come with me," Archie said, taking her by the hand and reaching up to turn off the bathroom light. As they climbed out through the remains of the door, Shannon looked at their reflection in the mirror. There was just enough light to outline the two of them in blue, shadow-creatures linked in the middle.

Archie led her to his bedroom, which she had not entered since that day she'd helped him move in. She stepped over some of his clothes, thrown carelessly on the floor and he pulled her down into the bed, still warm from his body.

For the first time, Shannon thought about what she was wearing. It had been her mother's, what she called a "granny nightdress." It was loose and billowy, patterned with little blue flowers and worn soft and nearly transparent. Shannon could remember being clutched against this very nightdress, her hair still wet from her evening bath. But she could not help but wonder how it appeared to Archie. Did she seem like some weird spinster?

Archie squeezed himself as close to the wall as possible and maneuvered Shannon until she rested inside his arms, her back and ass cradled against his chest and groin. This was by far the most intimate contact the two of them had ever had and yet Shannon found it utterly non-sexual. What she felt most was . . . ease. A kind of effortlessness, like pulling your feet up from the pool's bottom only to discover that you float after all.

She relaxed into him. His breath was regular and steady; it skimmed the skin on the back of her neck. The pillow under her face smelled like him. That was the last conscious thought she had before she drifted off into sleep.

For the first time in weeks, there were no bad dreams for Shannon Liao.

———o———

"I don't know if he'll take you, so you've got to understand that I'm not promising anything," Devon warned her as they stood up to go. "I don't know what your deal is but I know that someone once helped me so . . . I'll help you."

Devon looked over both of her shoulders in her in a ridiculous spy pantomime. "I'll give you a name, that's all. What you do with it is your business."

The older woman leaned in close to whisper in Shannon's ear.

Shannon listened.

TEN

CRY HALLELUJAH

The first person to notice the soldiers was, appropriately, one of the women on watch duty. She sent a runner (a weedy ten-year-old boy) back to the community property to alert Sylvie Solis. The band of soldiers was small—five men— and appeared to be only lightly armed. They looked like regular Army from their gear. That, in and of itself, did not exactly panic Sylvie. There was Fort Cowan nearby and she had long expected that, at one point or another, the military might become interested in an isolated compound so close to their base.

The second person to notice was actually one of the dogs. Sylvie's German Shepard mix Brandy alerted on one of the men, running through the woods and whining piteously at the door of Sylvie's yurt. It was a fearful sound that she had never heard the animal make before and Sylvie knew very well what that meant. At least one of the "soldiers" was actually a machine.

The man she now knew to be Edmond West had enlightened her as to the true—and terrible—extent of the Bots' capabilities, but she still didn't think that such a small number would be sent to deal with an entire community. The Bots would certainly be capable of attacking all of them, but might have more trouble containing them with a forest full of potential escape routes and more than seventy individuals to account for.

All of this suggested to Sylvie that this was a strike team, arranged and deployed for one specific purpose and Sylvie had a pretty good idea what that purpose was. Her radio had told her everything she needed to know about the relationship between Edmond and the United States Military: they were going to find him, hunt him down and take him . . . somewhere. Maybe just kill him.

The others were starting to notice the disturbance. The other dogs were getting agitated, people were emerging from their houses, setting aside their tasks and drifting towards Sylvie's yurt, the informal center of the community.

She stood outside, her hand on Brandy's head. The dog clung to her like a shy child at a family reunion. They were all looking to her, all these men, women, and children who had put their lives in her hands. Sylvie licked her lips. They were dry and her lower lip had cracked right down the middle. Her skin always dried out when she got stressed. She could taste blood.

"Okay, guys," she said, "we have an invading force incoming. We may need to protect ourselves so you go to your stations and get ready."

"That one . . . is poisonous." The little girl pointed to an orange-ish mushroom, rippled like an old-fashioned ruffled skirt. Edmond made a notation in the little pad of lined paper he had taken to carrying around.

"The good ones are tall, they look like rocket ships." The girl was, Edmond had been told, the very best at foraging. She knew the deadly from the nourishing better than anyone else in the community. "I have good eyes," she had told him, pointing to the both of them.

Edmond had to admit that this was certainly the truth. She had pointed out several leaves that seemed completely identical to Edmond, telling him that each one apparently had radically different properties. Edmond had never realized that there was so much in the average forest that could kill him.

Her hearing, apparently, was also better than

Edmond's. She stopped suddenly and stood up, tilting her head to one side and sending her yellow ponytail swinging crazily. "That's the dogs," she muttered, wrinkling up her eyebrows. "They're all barking."

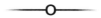

They weren't trying to sneak, which was for the best because Sylvie had people on all the reasonable routes into the community. Instead, they came right up to the informal "entrance" and called out for anyone who might be listening.

The dogs were in paroxysms of frustration, held back by grave-faced owners. They were protesting so loudly that Sylvie almost couldn't hear the man shouting at first. "Hello?" he cried. "We need to speak to Sylvie Solis!"

Brandy was glued to her lower legs as she approached the men. Sylvie did not keep personal weapons in her home, except for a small all-purpose knife. She came to them empty handed and tried to look as neutral as possible.

"That's me," she said.

The man who had called out her, the one who appeared to be the leader was huge and bear-like and he wore a very non-military half-beard. "Sylvie Solis, I'm Captain Prowsky. We'd like to talk to someone we believe is living here on your"—he took a slow look around the clearing—"property."

"That seems pretty irregular," Sylvie countered. "On whose behalf are you going to talk to this person?"

"On behalf of the US military, ma'am."

Sylvie nodded. "Well, I'm not going to be able to let you do that," she said.

Nothing changed in the man's face. He looked as though he had expected every single word that came out of her mouth.

"Ma'am, we don't require your permission. It just makes all of this a lot easier."

Sylvie was very conscious of what she was doing

now. She was gambling with the lives of every one of her people, people who had trusted her and followed her. To simply let these men take Edmond, however, was another kind of gamble, a gamble with the long-term viability of the community.

Sylvie took a deep breath. This was a moment for mettle. "Sir," she said, "fuck *easy*."

---o---

It was something that Edmond had never fully reconciled, how harmless gunshots sounded from sufficiently far away. Little insistent pops, like small fireworks. The girl didn't know what they were and she looked up at Edmond, questioning. She had probably never heard gunfire, except perhaps during some sort of target practice.

Edmond didn't look back at her. Instead he faced towards the community proper and squinted intensely, as though he could see anything at this distance. To go back now would be to put himself and the child in possible danger. To stay out here in the forest, though, seemed equally intolerable. If those gunshots were about him—for him—perhaps he could do something, address the situation in some way.

"Stay behind me," he told the girl. "When we get closer to the houses, put your arms up over your head and keep your palms open."

Sylvie didn't know who fired the first shot. She had a sinking feeling that it was one of her own people. They had done lackluster drills on this sort of situation, but she was dealing with people more accustomed to growing root vegetables than firing shotguns. It wouldn't surprise her at all if someone had an itchy trigger finger.

The exchange of gunfire was brief but intense. Sylvie herself ducked, half-crawling back towards the defensive line of the houses. She heard someone screaming so impossibly high-pitched and unending that she couldn't even tell if it was a man or a woman.

The percussive blasts of the guns up close rendered her half-deaf. She dug her fists into Brandy's fur and let the animal lead her back towards the trailers.

"Jackie, Jackie, Jackie," a woman—Loris MacPherson—was sobbing, half in and half out of a yurt. On the floor next to her was a teenager wearing stained jeans and a windbreaker. His face was too damaged to identify him, but Sylvie knew him just the same. Jack. Fifteen years old. His hands were twitching violently, as though grasping for something just out of reach.

Distantly, she heard one of the soldiers yell. The man dropped to one knee, it looked like he'd been hit somewhere in the upper chest or shoulder. For a moment, the firing intensified.

"Get behind cover," Sylvie shouted, pushing Loris MacPherson back into the house. She grabbed one of Jackie's shaking hands and dragged him in along with her. "Stay in here," she said, shutting the flimsy door and—oh, who did they think this would hold back?

Edmond's voice was like a cutting implement. It severed the chaos of the immediate past from the new, eerie silence of the present. "STOP," he yelled and, for a second, it was as if the entire natural world obeyed him.

Sylvie would swear that even the birds fell silent.

---o---

The little girl broke the rules almost instantly. As soon as she reached the half-circle of houses, she sucked in a huge, panicked breath. She darted away from him so fast, and, though Edmond stretched out his arms to hold her back, she evaded him easily.

She rocketed towards the door of a yurt and stood there, a tiny figure dwarfed by the shadow of the yurt's interior. "Jackie?" she gave a strangled sob. "Jackie?" more insistent now.

A woman appeared, shaking visibly. She wrapped the girl in her white arms and crushed her against her body. The both of them were sobbing and their tears assumed a kind of frequency as they shook together.

Edmond walked as close to the center of the community as he dared, he kept his hands above his head. He was shouting something, but he couldn't hear himself over the roaring in his own head. Whatever he said, it seemed to still them for the moment.

They lowered their weapons, but Edmond knew from experience that they could still fire within seconds, should they need to. "I am Edmond West," he said, loudly and clearly. He started walking towards them, each step deliberate and achingly slow. "I am surrendering. Unconditionally."

He reached the little knot of men. One was lying behind a half-felled tree and bleeding badly.

His face looked awfully white. The other four were eying Edmond cautiously. Edmond dropped his hands. "Your friend is hurt," he said, gesturing towards the shot man. "We should leave now and get him some medical attention."

One of the men, enormous and bearded, wore a flex-tablet around his wrist. He pushed his uniform's sleeve up and tapped something into the display. "Pat him down," he said to one of the others, a dark haired man with sad, deep-set eyes.

The man did so, turning Edmond around so he could check his back pockets. Edmond now faced the buildings and the people huddled in and around them. The little girl was fully encased in her mother's arms. Sylvie stood beside the both of them, her hand hovering in the air between them as though she longed to reach out to comfort them but couldn't quite bridge the gap.

Sylvie was looking at him; there was something stricken in her face. For a second, Edmond thought about shouting an apology to her. To all of them.

But instead he remained silent. When he was a child, his mother always used to tell him that, "Sorry doesn't cut the mustard." She told him that apologies only mattered if you could fix the problem.

Edmond could not fix this. He could not fix that boy.

And so he said nothing at all.

"He's good," the sad-eyed man said. The bearded man gestured to the rest of them and they turned, two of the others helping the injured man to his feet.

"Move out," the sad-eyed man told him, his hand at Edmond's elbow like a gentleman helping a lady take a turn about the ballroom. That hand was there to remind Edmond that, at any moment, this whole situation could get nasty. It was to keep Edmond docile. But Edmond needed no such reminders.

The fight had gone out of him long ago.

They couldn't get a vehicle in on that tiny little road, Edmond figured, so they were forced to walk out at a snail's pace, compensating for the wounded man.

"Which one of you is it?" Edmond wondered, when they had been walking for about a quarter of a mile. They did not play coy with him or pretend that they had no idea what he was talking about.

"Me," said the sad-eyed man, his voice especially loud as he was stationed right at Edmond's side. "I'm a Hart Series."

Edmond could have laughed or vomited. Instead, he offered this man—this machine—what he had denied to Sylvie and the rest of them. "I'm sorry," he said, utterly genuine.

The sad-eyed man did not react. Edmond eye-balled him as they walked. He was very well-made. They must have sorted out a lot of the kinks in Edmond's absence.

"You know," Edmond said, "you are the only thing I ever wanted, since I was a teenager. Maybe even before. You know who I am, don't you?"

"I know," the Bot admitted.

"I spent my whole life on you, on your kind." Edmond felt a laugh bubble up from some forgotten place inside him. The Bot looked askance at him as the laughter spilled out. Edmond supposed he must sound like an imbecile. "For years, decades, you were my dream. I thought I was saving the world and I want you to know that. Whatever else happens to you, and I'm guessing it'll be some truly awful shit, I want you to know that I meant well.

'Maybe you guys should consider yourselves lucky? You just got a hell of a lot more than any human ever will. Isn't it nice, for your creator to admit that he meant well but he's just an irredeemable fuck-up? Our God just leaves us to wonder."

The sad-eyed man said nothing to this.

They weren't that far from the community. If Edmond really focused, he could probably still hear the crying. Every single place he left, he left it a smoking crater.

"I admit, I'm a piss-poor god." Edmond wasn't sure who he was talking to at this point. Maybe just himself. Maybe he simply needed to remind himself that he had a voice. "But it wasn't completely my fault. These people," he gestured at the other soldiers, totally indifferent to his speech, "helped. If I had my way, there wouldn't have been any of this indestructible bullshit. How would you like that? Get some bruises and cuts, die when a thing is supposed to?

"You were all supposed to die. Or hurt. To suffer. That's why I made you, to suffer in the place of real people. I made you to be targets for the worst of us because I thought I could quarantine misery. I thought if I locked it all up tight inside of you, it wouldn't ever spread out and infect the rest of the world."

He didn't look at the sad-eyed man. He didn't see his face change if, indeed, it changed at all.

"I just want you to know," Edmond said softly. "That's important. It's important for you to know that I'm sorry."

He thought he heard the other man say something. He thought he heard the man say, "I know." But he couldn't be sure. He definitely heard the leather whisper of the man's pistol leaving its holster. He even heard the little rustling as the metal barrel parted Edmond's curls to rest, closer than a lover's kiss, against the side of his head.

The blast, of course, was too big to hear.